THE SHARD BRAND

Rufus Shard was born for trouble. The combination of short fuse temper, rattler-fast draw and a lust for power was a lethal mixture. So it was no surprise that violent death became routine when he took over the largest outfit in the territory. The Circle S bled the town dry and its boss dealt out death to anyone who stood in the way. Something had to be done. But who would dare to stand up against Shard?

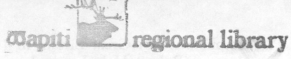

B. J. HOLMES

THE SHARD BRAND

Complete and Unabridged

LINFORD
Leicester

First published in Great Britain in 1996 by
Robert Hale Limited
London

First Linford Edition
published 1997
by arrangement with
Robert Hale Limited
London

British Library CIP Data

Holmes, B. J.
    The Shard Brand.—Large print ed.—
Linford western library
    1. Western stories
    2. Large type books
    I. Title
    823.9'14 [F]

    ISBN 0–7089–5053–1

Published by
F. A. Thorpe (Publishing) Ltd.
Anstey, Leicestershire

Set by Words & Graphics Ltd.
Anstey, Leicestershire
Printed and bound in Great Britain by
T. J. International Ltd., Padstow, Cornwall

This book is printed on acid-free paper

For Betty and Bernard

1

RUFUS SHARD was irritable. He was on a bad run. The money didn't matter, it was the principle of the thing. He just didn't cotton to losing at anything. He studied the latest in a long line of bum hands, then grunted "Fold," throwing the cards into the middle of the table.

"I'll tap you," the man opposite said to the one remaining player, who came back with, "OK, what you got?"

Three fours beat a pair of jacks and the winner raked in a pile of coins and bills.

Rufus leaned back, stretched and pinched his booze-bleary eyes with his hand. He and the boys had had a long spell in the saloon after a hard ride out to the northern end of the spread to chase off some settlers. He'd enjoyed

1

that: scaring the bee-jesus out of no-account nesters. The bozos had argued that they hadn't been on Circle S land; but that wasn't the point. No, sirree. Folks started settling near the fence, one thing led to another, next thing you knew, the fences were down and the outfit's beef was wandering all over the range.

He liked it when they mouthed back. Gave him the opportunity to throw some lead around and make a noise. Seeing the fear in their eyes, especially the young females, that gave him a kick. So what? It was their own fault. It was the no-consequence bleatings of the old folk that got to him. Sanctimonious dodderers.

So, the day had provided him with some funning. It was good to give the trigger fingers some exercise. But it had been a long ride out and an even longer one back. Hell fire, they'd ridden the skins off their asses and deserved some relax time.

But even boozing and card-playing

could lose their charms, especially if you were losing. He threw the dregs of the shot glass to the back of his throat. "I've had my bellyful of this place. I'm heading back to the ranch."

He pulled himself together and the other four hands joined him as he staggered towards the batwings.

Outside the sun was well on its downward path. Rufus watched the men walk towards their horses and prepare to mount but he lingered on the boardwalk. The bile had been building up and was still bubbling inside of him, looking for some way of getting itself syphoned off. He watched the men tightening cinches, gripping saddlehorns. Then his mean-slitted eyes caught sight of a Mexican stepping down from the boardwalk close by.

"Hey, you, greaser, what's your name?"

The Mexican was too near to pretend he hadn't heard. He stopped and looked back at the lurching figure outside of the saloon and recognized him. "My

3

name, it is Emilio Navas, *señor*."

Rufus nodded. "Well, Emilio, you Mexes are supposed to be happy-go-lucky folk. This hang-dog town needs brightening up. Give us a dance."

"I don't want no trouble, Mr Shard."

The bitterness in Rufus's features became even more obvious. "That's a mistake, bean-eater, calling me Shard." Although the name of his stepfather had been legally transferred to him when his mother had remarried, it had never sat well on his shoulders. He'd been born Hooper and that's the way it would be.

"*Señor*, I am sorry if I offended. Please accept my apology and leave me go about my business."

Rufus's hard expression was unchanging. "I said dance, you bastard."

The Mexican shook his head. He was a poor man living in the gringos' land but he had his limits to how far he would allow his dignity to be challenged. Besides, he was a lot older than this Anglo. These were the things that he wished to say but he confined himself to "Excuse me, *señor*," and made to continue crossing the street.

He only made two paces because Rufus pulled his six-gun and blasted sand inches ahead of his sandalled feet. Riders grappled to calm their startled horses while folks the length of the main drag stopped in their tracks to look at the cause of the explosion. The sound caught the attention of Sheriff Ruddock who was sitting outside the law office a spit's distance away. He took out the makings and built himself a cigarette as he watched the scene.

Silent, but contempt clear in his eyes, the Mexican stopped and turned to face his challenger.

"Well," Rufus went on, "you gonna dance?"

The elder man cast his eyes around the onlookers to see if he had any support but knew he would see none. There was nobody in town who would stand up to the Circle S gunnies. He was on his own. But if no one else would stand up to them, *caramba*, he would. He shook his head once more.

The blood disappeared beneath the tanned skin of Rufus's face and his gun racketed again. The Mexican's calf exploded redness and he collapsed to the dirt.

"OK, greaseball," Rufus sneered, looking down on the fallen man with an obvious satisfaction. "You're excused. Now you got a reason not to dance."

He laughed and looked across at the sheriff whose only response was to light his cigarette. Then Rufus sheathed his gun and tottered towards his horse. "OK, boys, mount up. Fun's over."

The sheriff watched them ride out of town, then spoke to a wide-eyed youngster standing transfixed on the sidewalk. "Get Doc Crane, kid."

2

THE man sitting stiffly in the stagecoach could have been anybody. His strong-featured face, with its tightened lips and glassed eyes, was a mask of impassivity. In the austere seediness of the stage interior, the short but stocky figure, in homespun suit, could have been a drummer or a businessman travelling to negotiate a deal — or maybe an old-timer blowing his savings on seeing the world. To his fellow travellers he had given nothing away during the journey, perhaps having learned the lesson that information revealed could be used as a weapon.

As the stage slowed in its creaky passage along the ruts of the main drag, he looked out of the window and knew he was back on home territory. His name was on half the stores in town.

Yes, for good or bad, he knew he was back in Concho Springs. He drew his head back into the interior and breathed deeply, gathering his resources for the physical exertions ahead. Leather brakes squeaked on metal wheel rims as the Concord lurched to a standstill outside the livery stable that served as the stage-line depot.

The first to alight was Dee Pascal, the shotgun rider. He slapped a farewell on the shoulder of the driver and dropped down. He had a pretty wife to get back to. Inside, the suited man waited for the other passengers to debouch then eased himself down. A man standing in the doorway of the stable nodded politely in turn to the passengers as they went about their business.

"Ah, Mr Shard," he said, recognizing the last traveller and raising his hands to the new arrival in greeting.

"Hi there, Amos."

"I didn't know you were coming in on today's stage, sir. Should have let me know. Pleasure to see you, sir."

Shard nodded. It figured he was unexpected: he had deliberately kept the details of his journey quiet. He stretched briefly, grunting as he did so, then took off his hat revealing a crown of silvering hair.

The ostler watched him fan himself with the hat. "Are you OK, sir? You look a mite pale if you don't mind me saying."

"It's been a long journey," Shard said, returning the hat to his head. He noted the stage-driver depositing a bag at his side, and pushed a bill into the man's hand. "Obliged."

He took a deep breath and nodded at the bag. "Amos, can you look after the valise for me? I'll get one of the boys to pick it up later. While you're at it, get me a horse saddled up."

The ostler, who doubled as depot manager for the stage-line, picked up the bag. "Sure thing, Mr Shard." For a moment he thought of telling him the trouble his boys had been causing in town a few days back but he thought better of it.

"And a canteen of water for the journey," Shard said. "It ain't the shortest of trips."

A quarter-hour later, John James Shard, head of the Circle S, was forking a large bay and heading out towards his spread. It was late afternoon but the sun still had bite and he intended taking it easy. It would be a good two hours to the ranch house. He'd hoped that by his return the weather would have broken. Green grass for grazing would be at a premium and drinking water for the herd would be scarce. Trouble with south-west Texas, you either got too little rain or too much.

The Circle S was the biggest spread in the territory. He'd had the foresight to set it up just as the railhead got established up at Abilene, and so his outfit had been amongst the first to get cattle up there to be shipped east on the newly laid tracks of the Texas and Pacific. He'd had his ups and downs but things had worked out well and the enterprise had flourished. Unable to have children of his own he had taken under his wing the son of one of his men who had died during a spat of trouble in the early days.[1] He had given the lad his name and raised him as his own.

As he rode he thought fondly of the boy, now a muscular young man. He looked forward to seeing him again, the one light in a life which had been darkened by clouds in recent years. He still thought of him as Buster — he couldn't help it — and chuckled to himself when he recalled how the young man repeatedly reminded him that his name was Chris, whenever the old man lapsed into using his stepson's nickname from childhood.

He remembered how the young

---

[1] The early days of the Circle S are recounted in *Shard* (Robert Hale, 1982)

Buster used to set up cans as targets for stone-throwing; the look on his face when Shard had presented him with his first horse. He remembered teaching the youngster the rudiments of cattle tending; the first time he took him on a drive to Abilene; how upset the lad had been when they had had to destroy injured or diseased cows.

The older you got, the more you looked back. But it was good to do that. Made up for a heap of other things: the bad times of the past; and the bad times that he knew were coming.

He was having these thoughts when, suddenly, invisible jaws bit deep into his innards. The doctor had said there would be pain. But he hadn't expected it to come so soon. That was why the laudanum had remained wrapped up inaccessibly in his saddle-bag. He couldn't maintain his posture in the saddle and clumsily reined in. He slumped forward over the saddle horn, then fell to the ground almost out of

12

control but just managing to stay on his feet.

Enfeebled, his forehead clammy with sweat, he hung on to the saddle to keep himself upright. At least he was out of sight of busybodies at Concho Springs, now some miles along his back trail. Fighting the instinct to double up his body in an attempt to squash the pain deep within him, he groped his way towards the saddle-bags. But he couldn't remember which bag the medication was in, and his fumbling with clasps was ineffective.

Hell, he didn't think that such a pain could get worse, but it did; and he collapsed to the hard ground before he could reach the bottle. For what seemed an eternity he writhed in the dust, his fists clenched, his knees rammed upwards into his gut. But in reality the eternity was less than a minute, for nature delivered its reserve balm, and he lost consciousness.

3

WHEN he came to he was looking into the face of a dark-skinned woman. "How do you feel, *señor*?" she asked.

Beyond her he could see a rough-timbered ceiling. He looked around. He was lying on a pallet in an adobe hut.

"Where am I?"

"You are in the home of Emilio Navas, *señor*."

"What happened?"

"I was working in the field. My attention was first caught by a riderless horse. I ceased my toil and investigated. Found you lying on the ground."

"How did I get here, into this bed?"

She smiled, exaggerating the creases in her leathery skin. "I may be a woman, *señor*, but I have strength. I managed to lay you across your horse

14

and bring you to our home."

She wiped his brow and he eased himself up onto his elbows. He felt drained but, thankfully, the pain had gone, save for a vestige of unease in his gut.

"How do you feel, *señor*?" she repeated.

"Fine, thanks." He looked around again. She had said 'our' when mentioning her home. "Where's your man?"

"He is in the next room. The pallet on which you lie belongs to our son Miguel. But he is a growing man and away looking for work. Do you feel like some broth?"

He looked at the window. There was still light. "No, thank you. I'd like to continue on my way."

"You think that is wise, *señor*? You still look weak. Maybe it would be better for you to rest awhile longer."

"How long have I been here unconscious?"

"For a while you were very pale.

15

Then much of your colour returned and you slept for about an hour."

"What about my horse?"

"Do not worry, *señor*. He is tethered outside in the shade."

"Obliged, ma'am." He remained silent for a few moments while he tried to assess his condition.

"You a local man, *señor*?" she asked.

"Just riding through." Although he was grateful to the woman he saw no need to divulge details about himself.

"If you have no place to go you are welcome to stay here for the night."

"No, thanks, ma'am. You've been good enough already." He swung his feet to the floor and made to rise but he became dizzy and slumped back to sit on the bed.

"Are you sure you will not take some broth, *señor*?" she asked.

He shook his head. "But I would sure welcome a cup of coffee if you have some, ma am."

"My pleasure, *señor*."

He watched her leave the room.

16

For a short spell he contemplated his surroundings while he waited to see if his capabilities would return. He heard voices. Someone, a man, was asking for coffee. That would be the Emilio she mentioned. He listened a little longer then rose. Finding there were no ill effects apart from a little shakiness, he proceeded to gather his belongings. He was used to feeling weak these days. He strapped on his gunbelt and, fixing his loosened tie, he stepped into the next room. The woman was hovering over the stove.

"I heard voices," he said. "Your man?"

"*Si, señor*. Emilio. In the next room. He is not well."

"What's the matter with him?"

"He has a bullet wound in the leg."

"Sorry to hear that. Has he been attended to professionally?"

"*Si, señor*. There is no infection but the bullet tore some muscle and the doctor says it will be some time before he can work again."

"Nasty things, guns. Nearly had an accident myself once when cleaning my rifle."

"There was no accident, *señor*." She shook her head. "My Emilio, he is a hard-working man. He does not look for trouble. But a gringo in town had had too much whiskey and didn't like the look of him. There were words and the gringo just shot him."

"You know who did it?"

"We know, *señor*."

"What action did the sheriff take?"

She chuckled humourlessly. "You are a stranger here. You do not know the situation."

"Will it do any harm for you to tell me about it?"

"There is one law for the Anglos and one for everybody else."

Shard nodded. "But I thought things were changing."

"Not round here, *señor*. There is a big outfit, the Circle S. It is run by an evil man. A Señor Shard. He owns the town of Concho Springs. The sheriff is

18

in his pay. It was one of the Circle S gringos who shot Emilio, so the sheriff, he did nothing."

Shard allowed the words to sink in, then said, "I see."

"It is a hell town, *señor*. The Circle S holds it in an evil grip. It is very bad for the ordinary people. The outfit owns many of the stores and businesses in town. They make it difficult for anybody else to start up in competition, so prices are high. And it is no better out of town. The Circle S riders chase off settlers. Fence off the land and stop anybody getting at water. We have talked about moving, but it has taken us a long time to establish our little homestead here. And, anyway, where could we go?"

At that point her husband called from the other room. Shard absorbed the information she had dispensed as he watched her pour a mug of coffee and take it through to the invalid. He heard the man speak; he knew enough Spanish to understand the woman was being reprimanded for talking too much to a stranger.

Accordingly she didn't resume her conversation on her return and he didn't press her with any more questions, just pondered on things as he sipped the coffee.

As he got towards the end of his drink and was gearing himself mentally for leaving, the woman left the room briefly to tend once more to her husband. Shard took the opportunity to take out his wallet. He counted off two hundred in bills and just had time to slip them under a jug on a shelf before she returned.

"Must be hitting the trail, ma'am," he said, as he grabbed at his tin mug and finished his coffee. "What do I owe you?"

"*Por favor*, do not insult me, *señor*."

He nodded and set his hat on his head. "Well, thanks for your hospitality, *señora*. Give my regards to your husband. Hope he mends quick."

She accompanied him outside and he eased himself up into the saddle.

"If you have a recurrence of your illness, *señor*," she said, "you know where our little *casa* is. You come back. You promise that?"

He nodded. "I sincerely trust it's not too long before your man is back on his feet." With that he touched his hat and gigged his horse.

As he rode towards the Circle S he pondered on the woman's words. There had been many things about the running of the outfit that he had not liked in recent years. But he didn't know things were as bad as the woman had described. Nor that his own name was reviled in such a way.

Although things she had described were not of his doing he was partly to blame. He had let things get out of control. In some ways he was strong, in others he was weak. He had made wrong decisions and had not corrected them.

Not long after he had adopted

the young Buster, he had met a woman while he was on business in Austin. Aileen. Aileen Hooper. She was widowed and had a son and daughter of her own, Rufus and Beth, both a little older than Buster. It was Aileen who pushed herself upon him. He revelled in the novelty of a woman seeking his company and he enjoyed the experience. Sharing each other's company took on some regularity and he began to think seriously about its permanence. The more he thought about it, the better the prospect of marriage appeared. He would have a wife — the woman was not without her physical attractions — and Buster would have a mother with a brother and a sister to boot.

There had only been one snag, something so insignificant to begin with that he had dismissed it. He had a housekeeper, Mrs McKinney. He'd taken on Jawbone McKinney and his missus way back in the early days. They were both a mite older than he and he had found he could talk openly about things with Jawbone. Whenever his mind was taken over by some scatter-brained project, Jawbone would bring him down to earth with a shot of common sense. With the passing of her husband, Mrs McKinney had taken over the role of father confessor to the ranch boss. She was closer to him than anyone, with no inhibitions about plain-speaking to him. And when Shard had mooted the idea of bringing a woman home, the old biddy had not liked the idea one bit, even before she had met the prospective bride.

"Facing facts, you're inexperienced with women," she had told him. That, he had to acknowledge, was true, but he couldn't see the relevance. So she had given him an instance, warning him the woman could be a gold-digger. He had smiled at her concerns and countered that possibility by pointing out that Aileen had independent means. She came from Waco down in the Brazos River Valley. It was rich agricultural land and her former husband had been big in corn. He'd sold up and become a prominent figure in finance in Austin such that when he had passed on he had left her with assets on a par with Shard's own. So whatever she sought from him, it wasn't money.

Mrs McKinney absorbed the information and let it ride but didn't change her mind when she met his wife-to-be, simply changed tack. Now the crux became she didn't like the woman for herself. "There's a hardness and a deviousness there," she had said. "You can't see it because you're besotted. Postpone any ideas about marriage until you really know the woman."

In some way the old woman was jealous, he had told himself. She saw him as a son, he reckoned, and he knew mothers could get jealous with another woman in the house. Accordingly, he ignored her warnings. Mere infatuation or not, he married his Aileen and for a while Mrs McKinney was proved wrong. In fact, the money angle that had so worried his adviser became even less of a concern when his new wife sank much of her own capital into the Circle S. The spread was expanded further, they payrolled more hands and the enterprise began to take over businesses in town.

For a spell that seemed to be the natural order of things but it began to rankle him when he realized his wife's plans far exceeded his own. He wanted something comfortable, something he could manage, something he could pass on to Chris and his other stepchildren. But she wanted more than that. She was an empire-builder. Seemed like she wouldn't be satisfied until she owned half the territory.

He had humoured her when she had insisted on vetting each of the new hands. They were man and wife and it did not concern him at first that the upshot of her involvement in the hiring meant all the new boys had allegiance to her.

And her aspirations went beyond

their own spread. The local town of Concho Springs was expanding. But there was no local government and the place sorely needed some law enforcement. It was Aileen who had suggested that the Circle S finance a peace officer.

That was the last major building block of her plans in place. She controlled the town and its law. So it was, that whenever someone tried to open up a new store in town the place got broke up, or even burnt down. And the so-called sheriff never seemed capable of nailing anybody.

Shard was finding himself at the centre of something he didn't like. As Mrs McKinney had said, he was inexperienced with women, and one of the things he didn't know was that a woman could seek such power. And that wasn't the all of it. As the years passed Aileen had become colder towards her husband. They had had separate bedrooms from the outset but in later years he had forgotten what the inside of hers looked like. Too late he had begun to see that he had been merely a pawn in her empire-building plans.

For these reasons he hadn't been the saddest of men when she'd died after a sudden and quick series of strokes. Of course, he had been unhappy to see her suffer and had done his best for her, arranging for a doctor to come in from Austin. Doc Fallon was a good man and stayed as long as it needed.

Each stroke had taken more of her capabilities but, mercifully, her illness had not lasted long. Shard had seen her passing as a release. A release for her from her suffering. For him, a release from her grip. But it was too late. He was not free from the effects of her machinations. The greater proportion of hands had been her appointments and the web of controls she had spun was entrenched.

He could have begun the process of dismantling it, but he himself had become weak, both in brain and body.

At first he had thought his condition was the result of the years of strain, and that it was just a matter of time for him to adjust to the new situation. That was before the stomach pains. And that was the reason he had gone to Austin to see Dr Fallon, this time on his own account. The prognosis had not been good.

* * *

It was too dark to see it but he knew it was there: Circle S land, Shard land. He was sitting on the veranda, the light from the kerosenes groping out into the darkness.

He had made it back to the ranch-house without further incapacitating bouts. Chris had not yet returned from the northward drive delivering cattle to the railhead. Rufus and his boys were absent too. He knew where they would be: downing liquor or parting the legs of doxies in some saloon in Concho Springs. If they were still capable.

Before dinner he had told Mrs McKinney of the doctor's conclusions. She was with him now, sitting close, her hand on his. They hadn't spoken for a long time. Two oldsters aware of their own mortality, staring into the darkness.

During the long journey back from Austin he had contemplated what would be her reaction to the news. Above all he knew she was the one he would have to tell. There was no hiding anything from the old biddy. 'Doctors can be wrong, you know, dearie,' he thought she might say. Or: 'There's always hope.' He had underestimated her. She had said none of these platitudinous things. She had pulled him to her ancient bosom and said simply, "We have been through many things together, Mr Shard. We shall see this through together too." And that was it. After a long silence she had cleared her throat of sniffles and said, "In the morning you must tell me everything the doctor has said about foods, about what is best for your comfort. And what he has prescribed for pain."

He was grateful for that. Thank God, she hadn't played the game of naive false hopes. Until eyelids became heavy the two of them listened to the night symphony of soughing breeze and unseen insects.

4

THE sound of a horse snickering greeted Shard as he entered the stable the following morning. The ranch owner smiled. "You miss your old man?" he asked as he made his way to the stall. "I'd have come last night but it had been a busy day. In fact, a helluva day."

Lancer was his favourite horse. Like his owner he had a mind of his own. Couldn't stand another critter near him. That's why Shard had had him installed in his own stable. Shard hadn't minded indulging his pal. He opened the stall and moved along the length of the chestnut patting its hide. It was still firm, the coat sheening in the morning light. The chestnut nosed at him in welcome.

A voice came from the door. "Howdy, Mr Shard."

31

He turned to see the stableman. "Hi there, Foley." Foley had been a pretty good puncher until he'd got a leg smashed up in a stampede. The ranch boss had kept him on to look after the stable.

"Lancer been OK?" the old man asked.

"No problem. Just come to feed him and let him out in the corral."

"OK. Just give us a few minutes."

"Sure thing, Mr Shard."

After Foley had left, Shard turned to the animal and stroked the velvet nose. "Well, Lancer, we been together a long time. Seen some hard riding. Been through a mess of scrapes but you never let me down." He remained quiet as he stroked the soft muzzle, his mind going over a shared past, a past that only the two of them knew. After a spell he winced. "The hell of it is I don't think I'll feel you under my ass again," he said, his eyes closing as he fought the sudden pain. He fell against the wooden slats, the torture taking the strength from his knees. But this time there was a reprieve. His face flushed with relief as he regained his upright position. When he was sure the thing had gone, at least for the time being, he took a currycomb from a box and began smoothing the animal's coat. He performed the ritual silently, lost in his own thoughts. Eventually he finished, patted the horse once more, then exited the stall.

He paused momentarily at the door and looked back. "Don't worry, pardner, when the time comes I know Chris and Foley will look after you."

He had left the stable and was returning to the ranch-house when Rufus and his boys rode in.

"Hi, JJ," the young man said, as he neck-reined his horse to a standstill near the old man. "When did you get back?"

"Last night."

"Where you been?"

"Oh, visiting old friends."

"Long way, Austin."

"Yeah. Need to get out once in a while. How have things been here?"

"OK."

"OK? Hear you gave some trouble to a Mexican."

"Damn greaseball was getting uppity." The young man looked across at the Mexicans' bunkhouse. "Surely don't know why you employ 'em. Lazy bozos."

"I employ any man who'll work hard for his dollars. Anyways, back to the matter in hand. I've told you several times before about causing trouble."

"We gotta show folks they can't push the Circle S around."

"The way I heard it, you were doing the pushing. You know what I think about that. I don't want any more of it. Understand?"

Rufus frowned. "I ain't a kid no more, JJ."

"No, but there's times you don't act like no goddamn adult."

Rufus glowered at him, then wheeled his horse towards the corral to join his comrades.

Two days later Chris returned from the trail drive. "See to my horse and rig, Deuce," he said, swinging out of the saddle and handing the reins to his segundo. He headed for the ranch-house and made his way to Shard's study only to find it empty. Then he scoured the place looking for Beth but couldn't find her either. He returned outside and crossed the hoof-pounded yard to the cookhouse where the flour on Cy, the chuck-wagon master, indicated he had already been warmly welcomed by his woman.

"Ah, Master Chris," Mrs McKinney said, espying the young range boss in the doorway. He put his arms around her and kissed her cheek.

"My," she said. "I know a young man who's in need of a shave." She wrinkled her nose. "And a bath too."

He grinned. "You missed me, Aunt?"

"I missed your noise," she said, a tone of mock rebuke in her voice.

He looked down at the cakes cooling in their pan. "These look good and smell better."

She tapped his hand as he made to extricate one from the dish. "You leave well alone, Master Christopher. Don't you remember how you used to burn your mouth stealing stuff fresh out of the oven?"

He chuckled, then asked, "Where's Beth?"

"Went out for a buggy ride with that Frank Turner."

He frowned. Frank Turner was a close neighbour. Too close for Chris's tastes. Owned the Hourglass, a small spread adjacent to the Circle S. Good-looking too, he imagined, from a woman's point of view: straight-featured with a pencil-thin moustache. And always immaculately dressed, like he was a dummy stepped out of a tailor-store window. Somehow didn't look right in the wilds of Texas. "She been seeing much of him while I been gone?"

"Afraid so."

"Why's that?"

"Well, she's been short of company while you've been on the trail."

He pondered, then asked, "And where's Pa?"

"Lying down."

His face serioused up. "Lying down? Is he all right?"

"Of course he's all right. We all need to rest up a little as we get older. You'll find out yourself one day."

After he had shaved, got out of his trail clothes and bathed he returned to the study where this time he found the old man poring over a document. Shard closed the folder so that the young man couldn't see it was his will.

"Chris. It's good to see you," the oldster said, raising a hand in greeting.

The young man looked at him quizzically. "You OK, Pa? Aunt says you were lying down."

"Sure. How did you do up at the railhead?"

"Great. Got seven dollars a head more than we expected."

"You paid the men off?"

"Yeah. Boy, did they show Abilene a good time."

Shard chuckled. In his younger days he himself had shared many such times with the crew.

"Brung most of the guys back too."

"Deuce still with you?"

"Of course. Best number two a trail boss could have. Fact, only a handful left the payroll. Got families to see. Expect 'em back before the fall. We run a good ship, Pa. Ain't many turn their back on the Circle S."

Shard smiled. He prided himself on that.

"In fact," Chris said with a grin, "you nearly didn't get *me* back, never mind the crew."

"How come?"

"Jed Stevens was giving me his pitch again."

Shard smiled. He'd known Jed Stevens for years. He worked a buying operation out of Abilene based on supply contracts with big eastern combines. Every time he saw Chris he offered him a job as a buyer. It was half joke but also half serious. Chris knew his beef, and Jed Stevens knew it. Chris would have been an asset in his line.

"Yeah," Chris said. "I might surprise you one day and take up his offer. Then where would you be, JJ?"

"Joking apart," Shard said, "you wanna think about doing something like. It'd do you good to work away from home for a spell. See something of the world. You've done no real travelling, you know. The world's a bigger place than the Circle S boundaries and the north trail."

"So they tell me." Chris's face became serious as he dropped into the chair opposite the desk. "You sure you're OK, Pa? You look a little thinner."

"Mebbe worry, Chris. I know a lot of folks didn't take kindly to the way your stepma conducted the business but I'm only just learning about the depth of bad feeling towards the Circle S. You know, for some the Shard name is dirt?"

"There been something happening while I been away?"

"A Mexican got shot up. As far as I can make out it was Rufus on one of his jags. He and his boys are worse'n a barrel-load of monkeys when they hit town."

"Mebbe he'll grow out of it."

"Grow out it? He's older'n you. You're loyal but a poor liar. I don't like to comment like this, especially to you, Chris, but he's turned into a bad un."

"I don't know, Pa. He's got his good points." They were empty words because Chris didn't know what he would say if the old man asked him what those good points were, and was glad he didn't.

"Suppose so. Deep down, mebbe. Anyways, what you planning on doing?"

"Well, it's gonna be few days before the fat ones start dropping their calves and the chores start mounting up again. So I got some time on my hands. I was looking forward to seeing Beth but I'm told she's out buggyriding with Frank Turner. Been told she's been seeing him quite a piece while I been away."

"Don't know about that, Son. I been away too."

Chris nodded. "So I think I'll ride into Concho Springs. Play a few hands, sing a few songs with the boys."

"You do that, Son. You deserve some relaxation after the Abilene drive. You'll probably run into Rufus out there."

"Tell me something new. Is he ever anywhere else?"

★ ★ ★

It was a quiet evening. Both main crews were in town. Shard was sitting on the veranda after supper. With Cy having volunteered for KP, Mrs McKinney

41

was free to join the ranch boss and came to sit alongside him.

She studied him in the fading light. "You're looking troubled, Mr Shard. You got pain again?"

"No. Just things on my mind." He paused then added, "I think I'm gonna have to sacrifice whatever feelings Rufus might have had for me."

"I don't know what is on your mind but it's time for plain talking between us. With regard to Rufus, you do what you have to do. You know he's a bad one. He has no feelings. For you or anyone. That's the kind of man he is. Why, the ungrateful wretch even rejects your name."

He nodded. "That's understandable. Encumbering him with the Shard name was merely a legal technicality when I married his ma. I am not his natural father."

"No, but when you married you did everything a father should. Treated Beth and Rufus as if they were your own. Treated them just like Chris.

Chris and Beth were in the same situation as he, fatherless, but they loved you. Still do. You know that. You've got two good ones there. Two out of three's not bad."

"Rufus wouldn't be normal if he didn't want to honour his true blood. I understand that."

"You're a forgiving man, Mr Shard. A man with a lot of heart. Not many of your kind about. Just like my Jawbone, God rest his soul."

"I had hoped that giving Rufus some responsibility would help him grow up, but he's interested only in drinking and gaming."

She tutted loudly. "And sporting ladies. You're forgetting that."

He shook his head. "And he's got a terrible streak of cruelty in him. Always seemed to get pleasure out of harming living creatures, including folks." He didn't speak for a while then resumed with, "You know . . . " But he didn't get any further. He suddenly gripped his stomach, abandoning his intended

43

train of thought and came out with "Oh, God," as he began to writhe in his seat.

She leapt up, gripped his shoulder, saying "Stay there", then hurried out. When she returned with a bottle and a spoon, he was doubled up on the floor. She managed to spoon some laudanum into his mouth. She stayed with him on the floor, cradling him until his body began to relax and she knew the drug was taking effect. She helped him back onto the seat. "Feeling a mite better?"

"Yes, thanks." He looked about the yard to check his attack hadn't been witnessed by any of the hands.

She dabbed away the sweat that had come to his brow. "You want to go to bed now?"

"In a minute."

She returned to her seat and he sat for a few moments, appreciating the effects of the medication. "Funny," he said, "when I was a kid going to sleep in my cot I used to worry that

I wouldn't wake up." His attack had taken his attention from their previous topic of conversation. "It's crazy the way kids are. I would stare at the dark ceiling and force my tired eyes to stay open. Now I have no such fear. In fact I look forward to it."

She nodded. "I have heard some call sleep the little death."

Hell's teeth, the old lady was a gem. She could have come out with some soft-soaping remark but she had gone along with his thought. He slowly got to his feet, and kissed her forehead. "But I'm waking up tomorrow," he said with determination in his voice. "I still have things to do."

She gripped his hand and held it tight for a spell before letting it go." "Night, JJ."

5

CHRIS was playing a friendly game of rummy in one of the town's saloons. It was good to see old friends, tell them about the drive, have a laugh. He didn't need to empty a beer barrel to have a good time. He could make a few relaxing drinks last all night. But even so, Nature made her requirements felt. At the conclusion of a hand he rose. "Excuse me, boys, the privy calls." He folded his cards and headed to the back of the saloon.

Outside he took a deep breath. He liked a drink but always found the smoke-filled atmosphere of a busy saloon a mite pressuring after a spell. The privy was just a dark shape but he could smell its reek. He stood there for a while, behind him the muted overtone of conversation laced spasmodically with a guffaw. He glanced up. The star-sprinkled sky was clear, no sign of the rain the land needed so badly.

Still conscious of the faint drone of voices behind him he pushed into the shack. But while he was concentrating on emptying his bladder in the trough he became aware of another noise. In the distance, not the sound of folks having a good time, more like a woman in distress.

Finished and back outside he looked in the direction of the sound. Along the alley he could make out shadowy figures. He advanced slowly, inquisitively, until he could make out the scene. A woman, her cries now muffled by a hand, was being held down by one man, while another straddled her middle. Anger surged up inside the puncher. There were some things a man just couldn't ride around and keep his self-respect. Now, sure of what was happening, he broke into a determined lope. Before the attackers were aware of his presence, he had leapt forward and grabbed the shoulders of the kneeling man, heaving him backwards, driving a fist into the side of his head.

Chris was a cowman, not a scrapper, but he carried muscles honed on pulling wayward steers since he was in knee-britches, muscles now adult and sufficient to pack a sledgehammer punch; as a consequence the struck man spilled to the ground like a sack of horse feed.

But before Chris could right himself to face the second, the man had let go the woman and leapt forward catching the intruder's cheekbone with a driving fist.

Chris collapsed under the crunching impact and, before he could rise, felt something slam into his ribs. Against the moonlight he could see a boot raised for a second jab. He grabbed the ankle and twisted it with all his might. The man yelped, lost his balance and crashed against a fence.

"What's that?" someone shouted in the distance. Oblivious of the voice,

Chris rolled clear and, in the one flowing movement came to his feet, just in time to receive the first man charging at him head down like a *corrida* bull. Chris took the impact and staggered backwards, wood creaking as his back slammed against slats. He struggled to free himself but the fellow had got him efficiently impaled against the wall. A second later the man brought up his head, crunching Chris's jaw with all the force of a piledriver. The shock momentarily wiped out Chris's defences and he felt hands closing round his throat.

He spluttered, wriggled, coughed. Unable to grab air into his lungs he felt his strength sapping and he dropped his hand, groping for anything to use as a weapon. Eventually his hand fell on his gun butt and he yanked it from its holster. Summoning up as much as he could of his flagging strength he whammed it against the side of the man's head. Then repeated the blow until the grip relaxed enough for him to pull himself free of the weakening fingers. Finally, for good measure, he cracked the man again, this time experiencing the pleasure of watching him fall.

But, out of his vision, the second had risen and was coming at him as he bent forward trying to get air into his lungs. Someone shouted "Look out" and he turned, awkwardly but just in time to see a fist swinging at him. He managed to move a little, thereby evading the full force of the blow. As the man hurled past, Chris added to the impetus by slamming the man's head with his gun.

Gasping for air he stepped clear so that he could cover both men with his pistol. The ruckus had acted like a magnet for the town's night owls and he became aware of an audience. A couple held lanterns and light spilled onto the scene.

"You OK, Chris?" It was Deuce.

"Yeah," Chris said, scrutinizing the two downed men who were increasingly bathed in light as the lanterns neared.

"Keep the critters covered and get their guns."

The victim of the initial attack had got to her feet and was standing against the fence holding her torn dress together.

Chris moved over to her. "You OK, ma'am?" he asked.

"Yes, thank you. They're animals. God, you arrived just in time."

Chris beckoned to one of the saloon doxies who had joined the onlookers. "Can you see to her, ma'am?"

With the woman in safe hands he turned his attention to the now disarmed attackers. "Spike, Arnie," he said slowly in turn as he recognized them. "Rufus's boys. I ought t' have knowed. Well, you've caused your last trouble in Concho Springs."

He took out his wallet, counted off some bills and dropped them on the prostrate figures. "I don't know what you're owed but there's twenty bucks each. That'll compensate you for any trinkets you've left at the bunkhouse.

You're off the payroll and I don't want to see you on Circle S land again."

"You can't fire us," one spluttered.

"I can and I am," Chris said. "Git on your feet. I want to see your asses on saddle leather and riding out of town — in the opposite direction to the Circle S."

He strode forward and pushed at the nearest with his gun barrel. "And I mean now."

"Put that gun away," boomed an authoritative voice. "I'll take charge of this."

Chris turned to see Sheriff Ruddock, gun in hand, forcing his way through the bystanders. Chris hefted his own weapon for a second while he weighed up the lawman, then sheathed it. "OK, Ruddock. The girl's pressing charges. And if she ain't I am. Then, when the law's dealt with 'em, they leave town."

The sheriff levelled his gun at the two men. "Like I said, I'll take charge and do whatever's necessary. Now, come on, you two."

6

WHILE he was shaving the next morning, Chris espied Beth through the window. She was in the flower garden by the side of the ranch-house. The Texas sun was no friend to delicate flowers especially in the hot dry season they were having but with judicious watering Beth had managed to create a colourful scene. He finished his ablutions in double-quick time and went out to where she was pulling out disfiguring weeds. She was bent forward with her back to him. He crept up and grabbed her by the waist.

"Oh, Christopher Shard! You frightened the life out of me!"

He kissed her cheek as she turned. They held hands for a moment gazing at each other. Many times during the past months while he had been away on the range her image had risen in his mind. Now before him in reality was that smile, the twinkling hazel eyes, the stray locks of hair. "Still pretty as a picture," he said. "Just like when I left."

"Flatterer," she said in embarrassment. She always reined in the conversation from girl-boy talk with him and this time was no exception. "Tell me, how did the drive go?" she asked in an attempt to change the tenor of the exchange.

He grinned at the familiar ploy. "I missed you, Beth," he persisted.

"I missed you too. Now, how was the drive?"

He gave up and followed her lead. "Hard work, then some hard work."

Her smile disappeared. "And the girls in Abilene, were they hard work too?"

"They were not for me, Beth. You know that."

"And what about the girls in Concho Springs. Couldn't wait to get out there, could you? Hight-tailed it out there as soon as you got back."

"No girls. Just funning with the boys after the slog back. Anyways, I asked after you before I plumped for going. You weren't around. I heard Frank Turner was occupying your time." He grunted. "Don't know what you see in him."

Chris had feelings for Beth that went beyond 'brotherly love' but being raised as 'brother and sister' put some kind of brake on his expressing it.

She looked at him and shook her head. "He's courteous and enjoyable company."

"And I'm not, I suppose."

"Of course, you're both of those things. And much more. But a girl needs some diversion."

He let it slide. "I see that dear brother Rufus has been running true to form while I been away," he observed, changing the tone. "I'm sure worried about the way he's going. There's gonna be big trouble one day."

"I know. I try to talk sense into him but it's to no avail."

"Sometimes I feel like he and I are strangers. We're not blood-kin but, I don't have to tell you, he means a lot to me." He thought about it and modified his statement. "At least what he used to be means a lot to me. We spent a heap of our childhood together."

"You don't have to tell me."

"You know, before your ma hitched up with my pa and brung the two of you out here, I had no playmates of my own age, there being no school and all. Can you imagine that. Two hundred miles from nowhere. Then Rufus came. City-educated, seemed there wasn't nothing he didn't know. Sure we had our share of butting heads. Hell, he beat the whey outa me a few times, me being the little one then. But he showed me how to fly a kite, play cards, whittle a piece of wood into a sword or gun. Took me on adventures."

He looked out at the prairie beyond the ranch-house and smiled. "We rode out there as knights in armour, led our own cavalry against the Injuns, played pirates in the creek. He was older'n me and I idolized him. Still do a mite, I suppose. Despite what he's turning into."

He looked up at the sky. "Talked to me about the things that only young boys talk about. Tall tales, you know, about adult things, silly stuff, but all a necessary part of growing up. He was the only friend I had near my own age. You think I can forget all that?"

"I think he has."

He shook his head. "Not deep down. He couldn't have."

"He was always jealous of you."

"What had he got to be jealous of?"

"You belonged to Mr Shard, and Mr Shard was boss. And Rufus was jealous of your relationship with the cowhands. He was the stranger, the interloper. Besides, I think they recognized the mean streaks in him even at that age." She sighed and surveyed her handiwork in the garden. Then she looked at her dirty hands. "Must clean up now."

They walked together out of the garden. Chris glanced at the yard and saw a group of hands who had just emerged from the chow-house. He stopped in his tracks and concentrated his attention on them. Spike and Arnie, the centre of the previous night's ruckus, were amongst them. "Damn my eye," he grunted. "Excuse me, Beth." And he strode over to them.

"Ain't you bozos got ears?" he snapped when close. "I told you pair last night you'd got the burlap."

"Rufus says otherwise," Arnie retorted.

"The hell he does. This was settled last night. Get down that wagon road and off the property — now."

"Leave 'em be, Chris. Rufus's orders."

Chris threw a glance sideways to see who was talking. It was Thed, Rufus's second string. "If you don't back outa this, Thed, you'll join 'em."

Suddenly Rufus himself emerged

58

from one of the stables. "You don't talk to Thed like that, Chris," he shouted.

Chris waited until his stepbrother had come near. "I'm in charge of the manpower, Rufus. You know what those two varmints were up to last night. They're animals, belong in a hog pen somewhere; and surefire not on our payroll. The only reason they ain't behind bars is because you've got the sheriff in your pocket. I should have known better than to leave the matter in his hands. Well, if we ain't got law and order in town, we sure got it here." He turned to the two men. "Now, for the last time, git while there's going."

"I won't allow it," Rufus persisted. "Spike and Arnie are my men."

"Huh, condoning their actions, you're no better than they are." As he looked at his stepbrother, he saw the determination in his eyes, a determination equal to his own. "Just back off, Rufus."

"I can't. You know that, Chris."

"Neither can I."

Rufus widened his stance in slow, measured fashion. "Then we'll settle this here and now. You got a gun. Use it."

"You know I ain't a patch on you in gunplay."

"Then you shouldn't be pushing so hard, Chris." Rufus took his time with the words. "You've committed yourself. Now go for it." Then he added in a mock playful tone, "Don't worry. I'll let you draw first."

Chris saw teeth through the smile and tensed his body, control gearing to a hairspring. As Rufus flamboyantly flexed his fingers, Chris suddenly bent and dived for the man's legs. Rufus was equally fast, his gun clearing the holster, but before he could do anything with it he was careening backwards, Chris's arms bear-hugging his legs. Chris grabbed his opponent's gun wrist and banged it repeatedly against the hard ground until the weapon fell. He then hauled Rufus to his feet by his lapels, simultaneously kicking the fallen gun out of reach.

Rufus tried to struggle free but Chris slung back an arm to drive a fist into his jaw. Rufus whammed backwards under the impact with his brother following through by leaping on him. The downed man carried a large sheathed knife but so energetic was his brother's assault that he couldn't get at the handle. They rolled around in a cloud of dust and Rufus managed to get in a couple of blows but they were ineffective. Fists had never been his forte.

The scrappers went on that way for another minute, the circle of onlookers widening to give the pair more room as they rolled over repeatedly.

"Break it up!" a voice suddenly roared above the sound of scuffling. Then, "Do you hear me? Stop them!" It was Shard, brought to the veranda by the commotion. Cowhands moved in and separated the two red-faced combatants.

"I don't know what this is all about," the old man bellowed when the two men were under restraint, "but I won't have brawling in the outfit. Not between hands, nor between those who are supposed to be bosses." He stepped down slowly and posited himself between the two young men. "Is that clear?"

There was something in his voice that they both responded to. They nodded, suddenly subdued by the man who, smaller than either of them now, had once towered above them when they were in knee-britches. He glanced at the onlookers. "And you lallygaggers — ain't you got work to do?"

The crowd broke up, leaving the three men alone outside the ranch-house. Shard looked the two young men up and down like a schoolmaster. "You pair, clean yourselves up," he said. "We'll talk this through over dinner tonight." With that he turned and remounted the steps.

Rufus stared at his opponent. "You've

shoved my face in the mud in front of everybody," he said, when Shard was out of earshot. "I won't forget that. You're top dog with your fists, always were. But one day we'll face up with guns. Then the play will be stacked in my favour."

★ ★ ★

That evening they took the first part of their meal in silence, broken only by a few pleasantries from Beth in a vain attempt to relieve the tension. As they waited for the main course, Shard studied the polished surface of the table before him, then looked up at them and said, "That was a damn fool action out there this morning. Throwing fists at each other in front of the paid hands. what kind of example is that? You ain't a couple of kids in knee-britches who can brawl in the dust. You're two growed men with responsibilities. You gotta show the right behaviour in front of employees."

"He started it," Rufus muttered.

Shard slammed the table. "There you go again," he snapped. "Talking like a kid. Hell, you got differences, you settle them in private. Preferably through talking. We got a business to run here."

He returned to looking reflectively at the veneered grain. Then he put a hand on Beth's arm and when he continued his voice was lower. "I've got a beautiful daughter who's never been trouble to any one. And I've got two sons who break my heart every time I see the two of them head-to-head." He looked at the two men in turn. "Don't you understand? I just want you to get along. For God's sake, you're all I have."

The two nodded.

The silence was broken by Mrs McKinney bringing in plates followed by Cy with a steaming hunk of beef. When the vegetable dishes had been set in place, Shard waited until the two older ones had left then asked Chris to carve and turned to Rufus. "It's in our interests to maintain good relations with the town. You gotta control your boys. That was a bad business last night. Now me, I want those two bozos to go. But you've had your spat with Chris in front of the men and I don't want to be seen favouring one of you over the other. I don't want the men to think that and, more important, I don't want either of you to think it. So Spike and Arnie stay. But, Rufus, if anything like it happens again, *you* gotta get rid of the perpetrators. That's your responsibility. Savvy? You've appointed yourself as the policing agent for the outfit; I've gone along with that because we both know you ain't suited to cow-punching and sitting at a desk makes you fiddlefooted. But a man concerned with discipline must be able to exert discipline amongst his own men. Understand?"

"Yes, JJ," Rufus said in a tone which, at least on the surface, suggested humility.

Chris passed the meat-laden plates

one at a time to Beth who doled out vegetables.

"How's the stock?" Shard asked Chris once they were all occupied with eating.

"Heard some scuttlebutt about an outbreak of cowfever to the west."

"Yeah?"

"I sent out one of the boys to check it out. He came back today. It's true. There was a drive passing through the territory. Got cattle tick. Started spreading to cows on the open range."

"No problem," Rufus said. "Me and the boys'll go and kinda persuade 'em they ain't welcome to trail through the territory."

"No need," Chris replied. "They've gone now."

"Any of our cattle die yet?" Shard asked.

"No."

"Good. Probably the risk is passed now. Nevertheless, keep a weather eye open. Especially watch where the breeds are grazing. They're our most valuable stock. What's the ratio these days?"

"About thirty per cent breeds."

Shard nodded. "Good. Don't let it get out of balance. Keeping a good measure of longhorns is insurance. I've told you, there have been those get-rich-quickers who have stocked out with Herefords and been wiped out. In good times the pedigrees give the best return, they reach full weight quicker and it's better meat, but they're as vulnerable as hell. The longhorn, she's stringier but she's hardier, don't need winter feeding and can look after herself against predators. The critters can go longer without water too, which is a boon in a parched up season like we're getting at the moment."

"Yeah, you've taught me well, Pa."

"This Spanish fever business — I don't have to tell you, the longhorns will be immune to the disease but our breeds could be at risk. Have you seen any signs of trouble with our stock? You know what to look for."

"I've got men out checking. Ain't found any symptoms yet."

"Good, But you hear of any more transit herds, don't take chances. Any signs of foreign herds close, have an early round-up. Bunch 'em on the east side, especially the class stock. Just to be safe."

7

THE following morning Chris looked in the mirror as he patted his face dry with a towel. The reflected visage with its bruises and abrasions reminded him he'd been in two scraps in as many days. But he'd given out more punishment than he'd received.

However, on one thing Rufus was right: the younger brother was no good with a gun. If yesterday's fracas had been seen out with gunplay, Chris wouldn't be now standing in front of the mirror contemplating his bruised features. At best he would be flat on his back, nursing some wound. At worst he would be flat on his back in a box. Rufus could sure pull an iron in jig time, while Chris had difficulty deciding which end should go in his hand. Odd in the circumstances, because his stepfather by all accounts had been a gun master in his day.

Over the years, from Shard himself and Mrs McKinney who had been with Shard from the founding of the Circle S, Chris had pieced together the story of his stepfather.

In his younger days Shard had earned his living as a hunter up near the Canadian border. As a consequence there was nothing he didn't know about guns and the shooting of them. But it was a skill he had been loath to pass on to his ward. Chris knew the reason. A few years after Shard had set up the Circle S, the outfit had hit bad times. However he had learned of the new railhead at Abilene and had been one of the first to figure that that was the way to ship beef out at a profit. He'd mortgaged and borrowed, to sink everything into hiring a top-notch crew and building up the biggest herd that had ever grazed the Circle S range. It was a last ditch attempt to get the outfit onto its feet. Then, on the drive to Abilene, the outfit was hit by rustlers. All the men were killed in the skirmish, including Chris's natural father, and the herd was stolen.

Shard had been left for dead and, badly injured, he was a long whiles recuperating. When he attained as much recovery as was possible he found himself with no men, no herd, no assets and the Circle S falling apart. Furthermore, the fact that he had been the only survivor burdened him with a wagon-load of guilt — despite his rough exterior he had a sensitive side.

There was only one thing for him to do, being the man he was: avenge the deaths of his men. That came first and foremost in his thinking, despite the fact it meant taking on a whole gang of hardcases. But, using his skills as a hunter, he did it. Tracked them, trapped them, and methodically wiped them all out.

Only then did he set about rebuilding the Circle S. He managed that too. But the sensitive aspect of his nature hadn't let him rest easy. Despite the fact that the hardcases had deserved their fate, Shard had spent the remainder of his life having bad dreams about the whole episode. Nightmares cartwheeling on the notion that he had been responsible for two lots of deaths. Not only the hardcases but he'd got this other crazy idea: if he hadn't employed the cowmen they wouldn't have died either.

So when he took the orphaned Chris, or Buster as he was nicknamed as a kid, under his wing he taught him everything he knew, save how to hold a weapon in his hand.

Now Rufus was a different kettle. When he'd moved out from the city he'd been enamoured with the 'Romance of the West', his head full of stuff from magazines and dime novels; and that meant guns. His mother had pandered to his every whim, including buying whatever hardware he fancied. The upshot was, after an adolescence with a gun glued on his hip, he was jim-dandy in using it. And that was why they both knew what the outcome would be if ever the difficulties between them came to be resolved by lead.

He finished his cleaning up and headed for the yard.

Shard was sitting on the veranda watching cowhands prepare for work. He'd had another bad night, knowledge of which he had managed to keep to himself.

When Chris passed him to join the men the old man stopped him. "Come into the study, Chris. Before you ride out, we've got things to talk about."

The ranch-owner rose and walked along the polished floor of the corridor, pushing open the panelled mahogany door. He eased himself into the chair behind the desk, exhaling slightly as he let go the tension necessary for the action.

For a moment he looked at his stepson sitting opposite, then spoke. "There's gonna be some changes, before it's too late. To begin with, the town's gonna be loosened up. I'm fixing to see to it that proper elections for town officials are organized as soon as possible. Most important will be a democratically elected sheriff. That way there'll be a law officer that everybody can trust, one who shows no favours. It ain't right that a privileged minority can do what they like, acting in a criminal fashion without being punished. Not in a civilized community."

"Rufus won't take too kindly to Ruddock being removed, sir."

Shard grunted. "That's the point. Shouldn't have been put in the position in the first place. Job's a sham, allus has been." He rubbed his chin. "Then of course, there'll be a mayor and town council, duly elected in a proper manner. If Concho Springs is to amount to anything as a town these things will come one day anyhow. May as well start now."

"There's gonna be resistance."

"I've met harder resistance than anybody round here can show me. In some ways I've been strong; but in some ways I've been weak. The set-up we got round here has been my wife's doing. I never could handle her, just let her get on with it. I built up the Circle S; me and those like me. Men like your pa, God rest his soul. But it was your stepmother who turned the outfit into a monster."

Chris nodded. "She was a hard woman in some ways."

"You don't know half of it, kid. Anyways I aim to undo the damage. We're gonna open up Concho Springs. We're gonna let folks set up stores in competition without hindrance. See to it that folks can walk about without fear. When our hands go into town they gotta know they gotta act like responsible citizens."

"Most of our men do, Pa."

"Yeah, I know, but there's a bunch that don't. Rufus's sidekicks. Then there's the running of the outfit itself. We're gonna negotiate water rights with those folks living on its borders.

Reasonable deals that folks will see as fair. If they're just starting up and can't afford to pay too much we won't charge too much. And we're gonna stop scaring the hell out of would-be settlers near our fences. Folks have got a right to settle near our borders. The region's gonna grow and we can't hold back the natural order of things."

"It'll be a hard rut to hoe, Pa."

Shard chuckled. "If that's what you think you got another shock coming. Your stepmother for all her scheming never wrote a will. Died intestate as the legal eagles put it. Huh, the old war-horse must have thought she was going to live for ever. Well, by the nature of things, with her passing everything reverted to me. If she'd thought of it she should have known she should have no worries there. Rufus and Beth have every right to their share of the spread, even though their mother's not here to protect the letter of their interests. The estate will pass to the three of you in equal parts as it should. My will is lodged with the family lawyer in town. As it stands the document doesn't say anything beyond that. But I been doing a lot of thinking the last couple of days. How could I treat Rufus right but trim his sails at the same time? I think I've got the answer. The upshot is, I'm gonna write a codicil to my will that will make Rufus a sleeping partner. He will retain all the normal rights of ownership with his third, he can dispose of his cut as he sees fit, but you will be responsible for the running of the outfit. Won't mean much of a change. I know you run it now, while he and his yahoos play at being cowboys."

"I don't know whether I could handle it, Pa. I know about beef, horses, land. You've taught me everything about the business. But I ain't too good with figures. You know the trouble I had with math at school."

"You got a head on your shoulders, son. You'll pick it up. From now on I'll keep you in the picture with all the accounting so that when the time comes there will be nothing you don't know about the running of the place."

"Mebbe, but that ain't the end of it. I know how to handle working men. No problems there. But Rufus's playmates are another kettle. They're hardcases. They won't take my orders just on a say-so."

"You underestimate yourself, son. You'll be able to handle that too."

Chris breathed deep while he absorbed the information. And it was puzzling why his stepfather should be having these ideas all of a sudden.

"They're on the payroll," Shard went on, "yet the only work they do is acting as a vigilante force round the fences or scaring off anybody who tries to set up business in town. And to them, that's just fun. They just take Circle S money and spend it on drink, gambling and sporting ladies. Not to mention ripping up the town when they get extra bored. It's about time that kinda thing was stopped. Anyways, I'm gonna be setting all this in motion before it's necessary for you to take over. It's just that I want to ensure Rufus doesn't have any say in its management. He'll have the same power-crazy ideas as his mother and that's got to be stopped before it gets a worse grip."

He lighted a cigar, a determined look in his eye as he studied the rising smoke. "I want to get the whole caboodle on a proper footing, while I can."

"What do you mean — while you can? You all right, Pa?"

"Of course I am."

"No. The way you're talking all of a sudden. These wide-loop changes to the place you're planning. There's something you haven't told me."

The older man's not answering gave the younger time to think, then he said, "It's got something to do with that mysterious trip of yours to Austin, ain't it? I could tell you weren't straight about your reasons for going. You just up and went." He thought some more, then said, "You went to see a doctor, didn't you?"

The ranch-man raised placating hands. "OK. I happened to see a doctor while I was there."

"It's more than that because it wasn't long after you'd seen the town doc here. Doc Crane said something and sent you to see some kind of specialist in Austin. What did he say?"

"I called in on Doc Fallon. You remember him? Looked after your step-ma when she was ill. He gave me the once-over as I happened to be in Austin. Just says I gotta slow down a mite, that's all."

"I knew it."

Shard smiled at the younger man's concern. "You might not have noticed, young 'un, but I ain't no spring chicken no more. Us oldsters have to slow down a bit. Nothing untoward in that. No cause for undue fretting."

"I'll find out. Mrs McKinney will

tell me. You always tell her everything. She'll know what this is all about and she'll tell me."

"Now don't you go bothering the old gal."

8

THERE were three bunkhouses. The biggest, largely empty at the moment, was for the cowmen when they weren't herd-driving or out on the range. A smaller one housed Foley and the Mexicans some of whom complemented the cattle crew while others did chores about the ranch. An even smaller building accommodated Rufus's gunnies, that is when they weren't hoorahing in town.

Like tonight.

They'd just killed a couple of bottles over a card game and were sitting silently in the semi-darkness. Arnie, Moses and Spike were content to remain still, eyes closed, in the afterglow of the booze. Only Thed was moving, playing patience with the discarded deck. His eyes indicated concentration but the turning and placing of the cards was mechanical; his thoughts were elsewhere.

Suddenly he said, "There's something wrong with the old man. Rumour has it, won't be long before he pegs out."

Arnie stirred. "What's the matter with him?"

"Something to do with his stomach I hear tell. You can see he's an ailing man. Face thinning. You watch him. Don't get around easy at all."

"Well," Spike pushed in, "if he's soon gonna be pushing up daisies, our troubles will be over. The Circle S will be split three ways. Rufus and his sister will have two-thirds of the outfit. That'll give the Hooper side of the family the upper hand. All the better for us."

"Shard is dying and he knows it," Thed continued. "And there ain't no way he'll let the Hoopers, and that means Rufus, take over, not as long as he's around to stop it. He'll do something about it before he takes his last breath."

"Hell, what can he do about it?"

"Ain't you heard of wills and things? I been watching him. He's been spending quite a spell of time in that study of his. I've seen him through the window a couple of times, looking at some official document. Figure it's his will and he's aiming to change it. All he has to do is cut Rufus out of the thing."

"He ain't that kind of a guy. Always was a bleeding heart. No matter how mean he thinks Rufus has turned out he'll still do what he thinks is right by him."

"Yeah," Thed agreed, "but he could put it in writing so that stewardship passes to Chris. That kind of thing can be arranged. Rufus would still have his share of the place — he'd be what they call a sleeping partner — but the running of the outfit would be in Chris's hands. And you know what that means: he'd run it like Shard would have done. Like the old days, everything above board. Then where

84

would that leave us? We got a damn good set-up here. We're riding a gravy train. The town's ours. All that'll go if Shard has his way."

"Yeah," Moses endorsed. "Might even strike us off the payroll."

Thed put the cards down. "That's right. I tell you, something's gotta be done about him before it's too late. He's gonna give the whole store away if'n nobody stops him."

"What do you mean — if nobody stops him?"

"You know how fix-headed the old buzzard is. S'only one way of stopping him."

"You mean . . . "

"Yeah," Thed said with an extra hardness in his voice. "Stop him permanent. Send him to hell in a hand basket."

With the bold statement of the proposition, there was quiet for a spell.

"We can't be certain Rufus would be party to that," Spike suggested. "He's

85

never been close to his stepfather, he's always made that plain, but he might have enough feeling to draw the line at rubbing the old buzzard out. Then there's his sister. She certainly wouldn't go along with such a scheme."

"Don't be a dumbhead," Thed retorted. "She wouldn't know."

"OK," Spike acceded, "I'm a dumbhead — but she ain't. There's every chance she'd tumble to what had happened and she'd give Rufus trouble on it. She'd come out of the events with a third of the outfit — just like the other two — and that'd give her the swinging vote on running things. Might even side with Chris. You know she's sweet on him. Who knows what she would do? I wouldn't put it past her to call in the law."

"We got Sheriff Ruddock in our pocket."

"She knows that, you meathead," Thed countered. "If she wanted the matter looking into she'd go outside the county. She ain't hard like her mother was, but she's got her mother's brain when it comes to getting things done. Concho Springs is a backwater. It's off the map as far as the authorities are concerned. The last thing we want is the county mucka-muckas getting interested. If they move in, the town'll be a dead duck for us. It'll have to be done so Beth don't get suspicious."

"And what about Rufus? Like I said, he wouldn't go along with killing his stepfather."

"He needn't know either. He'd be happy enough the way it fell. And that would be that."

It went quiet again for a spell while each man kicked the idea around, then Spike asked, "How would we do it? Ailing as he is, Shard's still top dog and got a lotta men round him. Chris and all the on-the-square cowhands. How could it be fixed?"

"Easy," Thed grunted. "An accident."

★ ★ ★

It was Arnie's boast that he could ride anything with hair on its back, but he nearly bit the dirt when his horse swung abruptly sideways. He, Thed and Spike were returning from a successful tax-collecting trip to town. Arnie had been riding a short distance to the side of his companions when the chilling whirr of loose bones in a rattler's tail had spooked his horse.

The sudden swerving of his horse had pitched him almost out of the saddle but, speeding away across the cholla-bedecked terrain, he managed to right himself.

To the amusement of his companions, whose own horses had been no more than startled, he sought to control his rolling-eyed mount. Eventually he reasserted his will over the animal and wheeled it round to return from his unscheduled detour. Stopping well short of the reptile that had caused the trouble, he dismounted, groundhitched his horse and pulled his gun. "If there's one's thing that makes my flesh creep," he said, thumbing the hammer, "it's goddamn snakes."

"Hold on there," Thed said. "Put your iron away. This gives me an idea."

Arnie reluctantly holstered his gun, still keeping his eye on the diamondback. "What's on your mind?"

"That action we talked about," Thed continued. "Putting an end to the old man's troubles. We'll make it tonight. Chris is out of the way, night-herding on the north range. And Rufus is aiming to go to town."

"How we gonna handle it?" Spike wanted to know.

Thed looked at the serpent, rattle now a low agitated whirr, its top section zigzagged back over its coils in preparation to lunge at whatever came in range.

"Spike," he said, "you ain't afraid of snakes, are yuh?"

"Give 'em the same respect I'd give any killer but I can take 'em or leave 'em. Why?"

Thed pointed to the diamondback. "I wanna get that ugly bozo back to the Circle S."

"Alive?"

"Yeah."

Spike thought about it. "Gonna need a bag. Gauntlets would be useful. But ain't no way a horse would freight it, no matter how you bagged it."

Thed looked in the distance. "No more than a couple of miles to the ranch." He turned to Arnie. "You ride on. Get a box with a lid on it; and a sack or two. Gauntlets if you can find any. You should find some in the forge. Bring 'em back here on a wagon. Don't tell anybody what you're up to."

"And a pitchfork to pin the varmint down," Spike added.

"Yeah," Thed went on, contemplatively. "That's the way we'll do it; gonna use that critter there. We'll get it back to the Circle S and keep it hidden. Then, Arnie, you'll go with Rufus to town for a night out. Get him crocked. Just to make sure he stays out of action, fix him up with one of the hurrah-girls. Give her a fistful of scratch to keep him occupied all night. When he's completely juiced, you ride back and give us the word."

"OK, but how you gonna get the thing to bite the old man?" Arnie asked.

"Summat more subtle than that," the segundo said. "Now you be on your way while we keep this diamondback staked out."

"OK, boss."

Arnie mounted up and headed towards the ranch while the remaining two took out the makings to occupy themselves while they kept their vigil.

9

IT was night. Thed and Moses were playing cards in the bunkhouse once more but their minds weren't on the game. In between deals Thed had gone to the window and surveyed the scene outside.

Moses had just dealt a new hand when they heard boots on the planking outside and Arnie heavy-footed through the door.

"Everything OK?" Thed asked, discarding the pasteboards and standing up. "Rufus out of the way?"

"Yeah," Arnie said. "There's no way he'll be back. Got so much booze inside him he wouldn't be able to sling a leg over a saddle. No worries there."

"Anybody see you come back?"

Arnie shook his head. "Nope." He glanced around. "Where's Spike?"

"Keeping a check on everybody's where-at." The segundo went to the window and looked through once more. Then: "Good. Here he comes now."

Spike entered and closed the door. "Cy and his missus have gone to bed. Beth's turned in as well. There's no light coming from the Mexes' place so they'll have hit the hay. Foley'll be with 'em."

"And the old man?"

"Still in his study."

Thed looked at the clock on the wall. Eleven o'clock. "So nobody's about?"

"Except for Foley giving the stable a last check, ain't been a soul about since sundown."

"Couldn't be better. OK, Spike, you know what to do."

The elder man took a deep breath as he contemplated the action, then left.

"OK, boys," Thed said, "we know what to do too."

★ ★ ★

93

Spike knocked on the polished door of the study.

"Come in." Shard's voice was weak.

Spike entered, hat in hand. The old man was sitting by the embers of a fire. He lowered a book and looked up. "Yes?"

"Sorry to disturb you, Mr Shard."

"What is it?"

"Lancer's restless. I was just passing the stable and could hear him. I wouldn't have bothered you but he seems real agitated, you know. So thought I'd come and tell you. Figure mebbe he might be sickening for something."

Shard closed his book. "Thanks. You did right, Spike. I can tell you're worried by the tremble in your voice."

Spike wiped back hair from his forehead. He'd hoped his nervousness wasn't showing. But if his boss thought it was due to concern for the horse then all well and good.

Shard rose with difficulty, wincing at the effort, and crossed the room.

"Wonder what's got into him," he said as he took his jacket from a hook on the door. "Well, let's find out."

He pulled on the coat and followed Spike along the corridor.

Outside Spike donned his hat and, as they crossed the open moonlit ground, he looked this way and that, apprehensive of being seen.

Meanwhile the three men stood in the darkness of the stable. Thed stood nearest the door, in his hand an iron bar used for firming corral posts. Eventually they became aware of the sound of feet outside, then Shard's voice. "Can't hear anything now, Spike."

"Yeah, he's quieted down some," Spike said, opening the door.

Shard followed him into the darkness. "Let's hope it's a false alarm. Anyways, better check now we're here. Light up a lamp, Spike."

The other walked further into the blackness, leaving Shard in the moonlight coming from the still open door.

Suddenly there was a figure behind

him. A raised bar fell. There was a sickening thump, a grunt, and Shard collapsed. Thed leant over him and landed another two heavy blows on the back of his skull. "Close the door," he whispered, "and get that lamp, Spike."

For the half-minute that it took Spike to fire an oil-lamp, the only indication that there were other men there was their nervous, heavy breathing. Eventually light revealed the crumpled figure of Shard and three men, temporarily inactive now the deed had been committed.

"Is he dead?" Arnie whispered, looking fearfully at the blood matting the grey hair.

Thed knelt beside the ranch boss, appraised the mess at the back of his head and turned him over. Shard's eyes were closed. The segundo felt at the throat, then pulled open the jacket to place a hand on the heart. "Deader 'n he'll ever be." He looked up at the others. "Now, don't just stand there.

Help me get him into Lancer's stall."

One opened the door while the others carried the body in and dropped it on the straw in the middle of the stall. The horse nickered and backed, stomping its hooves in agitation, as though aware that something was wrong.

They exited and Thed closed the stall door. "Spike, get the rattler."

Spike handed the lamp to Thed and tapped the shoulder of one of the men to help him. They disappeared into the darkness to re-emerge with a wooden chest.

"The rest of you, out the back way," Thed said. "Get back to the bunkhouse and make as though you're asleep. Don't put on any lights. I'll join you." He turned to Spike. "OK, do your stuff."

Spike donned some gauntlets and opened the box. Hardly muffled by the bag an ominous rattle was already reflecting the snake's agitation. He upended the box so that its content fell to the ground. With its undulating surface the bag gave the appearance of being some live thing itself.

Spike laid a booted foot below the neck and picked at the rope knot. With gloved fingers it was no easy task but he managed to undo the fastening. Folding over the freed end he raised the writhing bundle and carried it at arm's length to the stall.

Bracing himself he kept a grip of the one end and released the other so that the deadly creature spilled out behind the slats.

Already agitated, Lancer now whinnied in terror, kicking and stomping.

"Let's get the hell out of here," Thed said. He returned the lamp to its hook and extinguished it. The two men took the box and sack with them through the back door.

"We'll dump these behind a shack," Thed said. "I'll get back to the bunkhouse. You leave it a few minutes, then fetch Foley."

10

MRS McKINNEY went to the porch when she saw Chris ride with some of his men into the ranch.

"You heard?" she asked as he neared.

Even at a distance he could tell her eyes were puffed with crying. "Yes, Aunt. Moses rode out with the news." He dropped from his horse, handed the reins to one of his men for tethering and mounted the steps. He put his arms around the old lady as she fell sobbing against him. Chris gulped and held back his own tears. They stood that way for a moment then walked huddled together through the door.

After a short while seated together on a sofa, Mrs McKinney blew her nose, dabbed her eyes and said, "I've been telling myself it's for the best."

Chris pulled away from her a little and looked her in the reddened eyes. "What do you mean, Aunt?"

"At least it was quick. Otherwise he was heading for a slow, nasty death."

Chris nodded and took her free hand again. "I knew it. He wouldn't tell me, you wouldn't tell me, but he was very ill, wasn't he?"

"Yes. Got a growth that was incurable."

"That's what the Austin trip was about."

"Yes."

"Why didn't he come clean?"

"He wouldn't have told Beth and you because he wouldn't want either of you to worry. You know how independent he was. And he wouldn't tell Rufus, you know that. He'd faced most things in life alone and wanted to handle this the same way."

Chris clenched her hand harder. "But he didn't face it alone. He had you. I'm glad of that."

The notion brought fresh tears to

the old lady's eyes. When she had recovered, Chris said, "Where is he now?"

"Rufus has taken him to the undertaker's."

"Did you see him?"

"Yes. They brought him in here after the accident. Oh, Chris, he was badly messed up."

"From what Moses said it was Foley who found him."

"Yes."

"I'll have a word with Foley, then ride into town. I'll pay my last respects to the old man, then there are things to arrange."

★ ★ ★

The stableman was in the Mexicans' bunkhouse. "Spike came to tell me he'd heard a commotion coming from the stable," he said in response to Chris's questioning. "We went out there and found Mr Shard in Lancer's stall. The horse had had a rattlesnake bite. We had to shoot him."

"Was Mr Shard dead when you got there?"

"Yes. We found the rattler in the straw at the other end of the stable in the morning. Shot that too."

"How'd you figure it happened?"

"Snake must have got in and disturbed Lancer. These things happen. Reckon Mr Shard heard some ruckus and went to investigate. You know how he loved that horse."

Chris nodded.

Foley shook his head. "Hell of a way to go, being killed by the critter you love."

"Wasn't the horse's fault. He wouldn't have known what he was doing. You're a horseman. You know how they can go loco at the sound of a rattler. It's bad enough out on the open range but it would be worse for Lancer being trapped in a stall with the damn thing." He thought about it. "What time was all this?"

"Can't be exact. Don't watch the

clock. Must have been getting on for midnight."

"A bit late for the old man to be up and about, wouldn't you say?"

"No, sir. I've often seen Mr Shard's lamp burning late these nights. Figure he's been having trouble sleeping for a long time."

Chris nodded. Sleeplessness fitted in with his knowledge that his stepfather was ill. He moved back towards the door. "Well, thanks, Foley."

Beth met him outside. "I heard you arrive," she said.

They wrapped arms around each other, then Chris said, "I'm riding to town to see him. Coming?"

"Of course."

★ ★ ★

"Wanna see the old man," Chris said.

The funeral director nodded. "Yes, sir. Just wait one moment, if you will."

There was a black curtain suspended

from a brass rail masking the rear of the parlour and the man disappeared behind it, leaving Chris and Beth to stand, apprehensive, aware of the strange, chemical smell. Seconds later the fellow reappeared and held back the curtain. "This way, sir, madam."

Chris took off his hat and they allowed themselves to be ushered through.

Shard was in a box wearing a suit Chris didn't recognize. Face was different too. Cheeks gaunter, closed eyes, sunken; face powdered white, cheeks reddened, doll-like. Despite the powder bruising was still visible under it.

Behind him there was a gasp from Beth and she quietly left to cry outside. His own eyes suddenly moistening he stepped closer and put a hand on the coffin's side. His stepfather had not been the tallest of man and in his growing Chris had soon become taller but in his final sleep the old man looked even smaller than Chris remembered. He said a silent goodbye to the man he had known as father, then headed back to the curtain.

Outside he rejoined Beth and breathed deep to get rid of the formaldehyde in his nostrils.

He settled his hat back on his head and was untying Beth's reins when he saw the saloon across the way and something occurred to him. "Would you stay with the horses a moment?" he said. "Won't be long."

He'd got that look that she knew of old telling he wanted to be alone. "Of course. Take as long as you like."

He walked slowly across the main drag and into the saloon. He ordered two drinks, a beer and a shot glass with a finger of pure alcohol in it. At a table he took a swig of the beer then put a match to the alcohol so that it glowed in front of him like a little candle.

The few occupants of the room observed the ritual with wide-eyed curiosity but he ignored them. As a kid he'd heard a tale about a stranger who had ridden into some nameless town to the north. He'd been driving a small wagon with a young boy on the box beside him. Leaving the boy he'd gone into the saloon and ordered a bottle of soda pop and nine glasses of the nearest thing the barkeep had got to pure alcohol. According to the tale the man had drunk one, then set alight to the other eight. Then left without a word of explanation save to instruct the barkeep to let them burn out.

The account was one of those tall tales you heard around the campfire and, although the story didn't carry the man's name, Chris knew that man had been Shard and that he'd been the young freckled kid on the wagon. He remembered the day Shard broke a journey with him at a cluster of buildings in the middle of nowhere; and he remembered him shortly coming from a saloon with a bottle of soda pop. Although he was a mud-and-dungarees youngster he had cause to remember that day because that was the day

Shard had told him his father was dead. His father had been one of nine Circle S hands murdered by rustlers; and Shard, stumpy, small-framed Shard had avenged them all.

Then the old man had taken the little Buster back to the Circle S and raised him as his own son.

In the saloon in Concho Springs Chris, the grown-up Buster, looked at the flickering flame, saw the sides blackening and remembered things. Good things. With his own father gone there couldn't have been a better man to step into his boots than the man now laid out in the funeral parlour. He'd had his funny ways but he had been a good man. As square as they come.

Suddenly the glass broke scattering the remains of the burning liquid on the table. He took another swig from his glass leaving a couple of inches of beer with which he put out the small conflagration. "Sorry about that," he said to the barkeep as he rose and moved away from the hissing spectacle.

"Don't worry, Mr Shard," the barkeep said.

Chris returned once more to the boardwalk, looked up and addressed a thought to the sky. You were in there with me, weren't you? Breaking that glass was your way of saying goodbye.

Then he rejoined Beth.

★ ★ ★

It was late afternoon at the ranch and Chris paid a visit to the kitchen to get himself a bite to eat. Deuce and a couple of cowhands were already under Mrs McKinney's feet with the same idea.

"Ah, Chris," she said when she saw the trail boss. "I was hoping to see you. Come and help me feed the chickens."

He looked at the inviting cookies and grunted dismissively. "You don't need me to help you feed the chickens!" He picked up a cookie. "Besides, I've got things to do."

"Chris, I don't ask you to do much now that you're a growed man but I am asking you to come help me feed the birds."

There was an insistence in her voice that he hadn't heard for a long time. Equally insistent was the hand she put on his arm to turn him towards the door. "OK, Aunt," he capitulated, hastily devouring the cookie. "Where's the feed?"

"Where it's always been since you were in knee-britches: in the out-shed."

She followed him outside. Minutes later they were beside the chicken run, throwing seed over the wire fence. She looked around, checked they weren't being overheard, then said, "What you planning on doing about the estate?"

"What do you mean — planning? JJ's instructions will be in the will at the lawyer's in town. When we've heard the reading, Rufus, Beth and myself will have to make decisions accordingly."

"Haven't you given any thought to Mr Shard's intentions? You don't have to hear the will read to know what's in it. The document will split ownership *and management* between the three of you. As far as ownership is concerned that's what JJ wanted but you also know that he wanted the *management* to be in your hands."

"That notion didn't get beyond discussion. He mooted the idea to me, but no decision was made. And certainly the will wasn't altered. JJ never went to town again before the accident. And it's the will and what's written in it that counts."

"I don't know about the law, Master Chris, but I do know what Mr Shard wanted. He won't rest easy in his grave if Rufus has a dominant say in the running of the place. Irrespective of what the will says Mr Shard wanted you to have overall control. He hated the way the outfit had changed. Taking over the town. The Circle S lording it over everybody, telling Sheriff Ruddock what to do. Squeezing folk dry. Not to mention the brutality. It was breaking his heart and he aimed to do something about it before it was too late."

"I know all that, Aunt Mary, but it's out of my hands. The law's the law. Things have to be in writing and sworn to."

"I'm an old homestead woman. Don't know much about the ways of the law and such. But I have heard that wills can be contested. If you got any feeling for the old man and his memory I think you should at least make a stand."

"How can I do that?"

"Get the name of a good lawyer. Somebody well away from Concho Springs, somebody who can't be got at by Rufus. Go to see him, ask his advice about contesting the will. Tell him the situation: what Mr Shard wanted, what he told you, the wishes he expressed to you. And tell him that Cy and I will corroborate Mr Shard's intentions. He shared many thoughts with us. We'll swear on oath about what we knew of Mr Shard's worries and his intention to change the will. Our sworn statements must have some standing."

"Doubt it."

"Well, I think you owe it to the old man's memory to do something."

11

THE mid-morning sun beat down on Chris's bare head as he stood before the grave. The preacher droned on, his tone somnolent with routine. Beth and Mrs McKinney looked visibly moved, as did Cy. But Rufus remained impassive, betraying no feeling save probably boredom. Deuce in cleaned-up range gear stood respectfully behind the main party along with a handful of the cowhands but there were none of Rufus's crew.

Chris was glad a man couldn't be around to see his own funeral. Ten years ago the whole town would have turned out to see him off; he had been a well-respected man. Today the name of Shard meant the Circle S and that odious label meant oppression. Of course, folk had looked from behind curtains as the pitifully small cortege had passed but apart from the family members and close associates the only outsider in attendance was Sheriff Ruddock. And he was only there because the outfit financed his meal ticket.

It stuck in Chris's craw that JJ's esteem should be so low. If it hadn't have been for Old Man Shard there would be no town to speak of. And certainly no population to justify the building of the white clapperboard church behind them. He'd heard tell that JJ had made a big donation towards its foundation. Couldn't remember who had told him. Probably Mrs McKinney. It wasn't the kind of thing he would have heard from the old man's lips. Made no never-mind; nobody would remember his contribution today.

JJ had been a hard worker and fair in his business dealing. But now, all that stood for nothing.

After the service the family group called at the lawyer's for the reading of the will. A simple document as expected. Apart from sums to the McKinneys and to the church, the outfit was passed jointly, lock stock and barrel to the three young ones.

★ ★ ★

"Hey, you remember the time we almost burned the barn down?" Chris said. He and Beth were reminiscing on the veranda, drinks in hand, still in their dark clothes following the morning's proceedings.

She smiled. "And Ma said it was your fault. She always put her finger on you as the one leading her precious Rufus astray."

Chris chuckled. "Yeah. I was the rough, unlettered urchin. Rufus was the gentleman from the big city."

"If things were ever that way, they've certainly changed. It's not fancy education that makes a gentleman. Whatever finesse Rufus ever had he lost long ago. Drinking, womanizing, causing trouble in the town with his pack of no-goods. Hasn't got a decent day's work in him. Ma started the rot. Spoiled him for as long as I can remember. She just couldn't see her boy doing wrong. If she were alive today she'd make excuses for him. She was blind in that regard. By the same token she treated you unkindly in many ways."

"Water under the bridge. Anyways, wasn't really her fault. Didn't take wholly to life out here. When she chewed me out, I just saw it as being the way stepmothers were supposed to be. You know, from kids' story books."

Beth shook her head. "Yes, she was the wicked stepmother in some ways. And she wasn't a good influence on the Circle S in the later days. With her big ideas of branching out, expanding, virtually taking over the town."

"Yeah, that was a bad step, I must admit. Goes a long way to being the root of the problems we have today. That's what Pa was wanting

116

to reverse before he died."

He could have continued the vein of talk but there were footsteps behind them and he turned to see Rufus.

"When you've finished, Chris," he said, "we've got some talking to do."

Chris nodded, finished his drink and raised his eyebrows exaggeratedly so that only his sister could see. "Excuse me, Beth," he said and followed his stepbrother.

Rufus closed the door of the study behind them. "Two-thirds of the Circle S are in the hands of the Hooper side of the family," he began. "It's unfortunate it should happen the way it did, dreadful business, but anyways, it means *we* shall be running the show from now on. In the circumstances it's only right that I should be manager of the outfit."

"You talked this through with Beth?"

"She's Hooper blood. Naturally she goes along with me. So, effectively, your dearly beloved stepbrother is in charge."

The listener shrugged his shoulders. Seemed damn-all he could do about it. "Reckon I have no option but to accept that," he said.

"Chris. You're a regular guy. Always have been." The new manager strutted round the room. "As to practicalities, you will be in charge of all matters to do with beef handling: round-ups, breeding, hiring and firing cattle crews, trailbossing up to the railhead. You're the best cowman in the Panhandle. And in the overall business, you'll be second only to me. Hell, we've grown up together. We can handle this together."

Chris had his doubts on that score but said nothing.

"You'll see," Rufus concluded, "between us we'll see the Circle S achieving even greater prosperity."

★ ★ ★

The next day Beth rode alone into Concho Springs to see the family

118

lawyer. She'd heard of Chris being given second place and wanted to know the legal position.

"It was Mr Shard's wish that Chris be overall manager of the Circle S," she said.

The lawyer shrugged. "He didn't alter his will to that effect. The estate is divided equally between the three of you. So, whoever is to be manager is to be decided by the three of you. I can't see the problem."

"But Mr Shard told me he wished for Chris to be in charge."

"He actually told you?"

"Not in so many words but from the way he talked there was clear implication that those were his thoughts."

"I'm afraid whatever he told anyone in private, directly or by implication, stands for nothing in law. The property is split three ways. That means the choice is yours. You can side with Rufus or Chris. Yours is the casting vote. Whichever you decide, that marks who will be manager. If you want Christopher in place you merely have to vote accordingly."

"It's an intolerable decision. Much as I prefer Chris for the job I can't decide against my blood brother. I am older than Rufus. It was always my lot to look after him. Make sure he didn't get into too many scrapes. Before Mother died she made it plain I should continue looking after his interests. Made me swear to it. I can't act against her wishes. I know it would be for the good to side with Chris but I couldn't do it and feel right in myself. Not with the commitment I made to Mother."

"Well, as I said, miss, the choice is yours."

She rose from her chair. "Well, if that is all there is to be said."

The lawyer sprang up and opened the door for her. "Having said that the decision is yours may I offer one piece of advice, off the record? More of a warning. We both know of Rufus's, shall we say strength of will, and that there could be consequences if you were to cross him."

"I'm his sister. You don't have to tell me."

12

"**H**ELL, what's he coming to sell?"

It was some days after the funeral and Rufus was going through his daily ritual of dismantling and oiling his Colt .45. To catch the light he was standing near the study window and had looked out to see the preacher drawing up in his buggy. "Go and see what the Biblethumper wants, Thed."

The segundo followed the order, leaving Rufus eying his stepbrother quizzically. A few seconds later the preacher came through the door. "Good day to you, gentlemen. Forgive this intrusion."

"OK, what can I do for you, Rev?" Rufus asked, laying down his weapon parts and picking up a cloth to wipe his hands.

"This is not a pleasant visit but I

feel I have to make it."

"Go on."

"There are some occupations where a fellow gets to know the feelings of a community, the keeper of a General Stores, for example. Mine's another. Folk open up their hearts to me. After what I been hearing I have come to speak with you in your capacity as manager of the Circle S."

"The manager of the Circle S is listening," Rufus said, dropping into the chair behind the desk.

"I come to speak on behalf of 'the hewers of wood and drawers of water'."

Rufus nodded in recognition of the words. "Joshua."

"You know your Bible," the preacher smiled. "That is a good sign."

"Got sent to Bible class as a kid. Don't bank on it meaning anything. Growing up knocked it all outa me. Now tell me what this is all about."

"Truth of the matter is, folk don't know which way to turn under the grip of the Circle S. I'm going to talk frankly: the way you stifle the competition and extract taxes from the remaining businesses. Many of the people were hoping for some changes after Mr Shard's death."

"I'd like you to know, JJ didn't initiate those arrangements in the first place," Chris corrected.

Rufus glowered at his stepbrother, then looked back at their visitor. "You ain't been in these parts long, have you, Preacher?"

"Long enough to realize I have an unhappy flock."

"Yeah, but not long enough to understand the situation. You see I am my mother's son. When she brought us out here, the Circle S was a one-horse outfit."

"Garbage," Chris countered. "It was the biggest in the territory."

"Yeah," Rufus snorted, "at a time when there was nothing else. Not even a town, just a bunch of soddies."

Chris let it ride.

"It was my ma," Rufus continued,

"with the capital she brought with her from Austin, who saw to it that both the outfit and the town grew to what they are today. Now, I ain't denying Old Man Shard had a good side. He took me and Beth in. You remember Beth? You saw her at the funeral."

The preacher nodded.

"Well, Old Man Shard treated us pretty much as his own kids. I ain't taking that away from him. But he wasn't my blood father and I've always known that I wasn't like him. I knew that when it was eventually time for me take over the reins of the spread I would change everything he did. Just like my dear departed mother I want to see the Circle S grow to greater heights. So we shall extend Ma's policy of making sure that the Circle S stamp is on every new business in town."

"Folk were hoping there would be changes for the better."

"Well, there are gonna be changes all right. Those businesses which we don't own shall have their taxes doubled."

"This is shocking. You are going to submit them to further exploitation?"

"Exploitation? That's a ten-dollar word if ever I heard of one. We ain't talking about exploitation here. No, we're talking about — how shall I say? — managed business affairs."

"Merely fancy words for exploiting the weak," the preacher said.

Rufus leant back in his chair and studied the visitor. "Your coming here makes me think. The church don't pay any taxes yet. Maybe it should pay its fair share like the others."

"That'd be going too far, Rufus, and you know it," Chris snapped.

Still looking at the preacher Rufus nodded his head at Chris. "You will note my stepbrother has more than a smack of the old man's influence in him. As I was saying, the town was founded on the back of the Circle S and the outfit has always taken upon itself the responsibility for law and order; and for managing the health of the town's business community. The Circle S will pick up that heavy mantle. But it is a fact of life that such an onerous task has to be paid for. In this world, ain't nothing for nothing."

"Already there is much ill-feeling in the town against the Circle S," the preacher replied. "If you carry out these ideas you'll risk having the entire town against you. I would have thought in your own interests that was a bad thing."

Rufus flicked a hand at his segundo. "Thed. Ride into town with some of the boys and tell those that need to know what I have said. Doubling of taxes. The policy is implemented as of now. And make it clear what will happen to anybody who has the notion to butt heads over this. Spread the word that for their own sakes they gotta forget Shard and his weakness. I'm in charge now."

"OK, boss," Thed said and made for the door.

The pallored face of the preacher had whitened even further. "Is there nothing I can say to stop you wreaking this unhappiness?"

Rufus smiled. "There's nothing more you can say to me, Preacher — other than goodbye."

The man of the cloth moved to the door. "Those who stake their fortunes on the evil doings of the Circle S will do well to remember some words in Ecclesiastes: 'To everything there is a season'."

Rufus's smile became a scathing laugh. "Hey, there is something you can say. In your next sermon to your precious flock, use Apostles as your text. Tell 'em 'It is more blessed to give than receive'!"

★ ★ ★

It was the day after the preacher's visit and word had circulated about the Circle S's increased demands on the town. Rufus was leaning on the corral rail watching one of the Mexican vaqueros breaking a new horse. Beth espied him from her garden and crossed the yard to join him.

"I've heard about the bigger squeeze you're putting on the stores in town."

"That's business, dear sister. No need to worry your pretty head about that."

"Well, I'm going to tell you what your friends won't: you're pushing the townsfolk too far."

"Hellfire, woman. You're as bad as that damn preacher."

"If you keep pushing and squeezing, who knows what will happen? The least you're going to do is kill off the town. And you'll make increased enemies."

"Oh, you're suddenly interested in my health?"

"I'm simply telling you you're making bad decisions."

"So my sister figures it's time to give me a sermon? Well, let me remind you, your little brother can't be ordered about anymore. I'm grown up. And I'm the manager of the whole shebang. I do as I wish."

"And that wish is to destroy everything that Mr Shard built, the town along with it."

"Huh, he was weak. This place was nothing till Ma took over, put him in his place."

"You're wrong. It was something. He built it from nothing. Nothing. There was just wilderness here. It had its ups and downs but eventually he got it onto a sound footing. Then, its success brought into existence the town; and then its flourishing in turn. But Mother saw it as something else. Something which could be even bigger. Much bigger. In fact, too big for its own health. You say I haven't inherited Ma's flair for business but I know one thing: there's a natural size to things. This was a cattle ranch. She wanted to make it the centre of an empire that dominated the whole territory. That role is too much for one enterprise. Nobody on the Circle S, including you, knows about running stores, saloons and other businesses. Our role was cattle and we had the expertise for it. Mr Shard, Chris. And the best crews around."

"The income from beef goes up and down. Even when the market's good, there ain't any fortunes to be made. The rock solid part of the Circle S's income comes from the town. Our own businesses and the levies we impose on others. You benefit from that, you know!" He grabbed at her shirt and partly pulled it away from her waist, maintaining his grip on it. "Look at that. Ain't cheap calico or homespun. Expensive material. Where do you think the money comes from to pay for that and those clothes in your wardrobe? Don't take the goodies and then complain about where the dough comes from."

She wrenched the material free and tucked it back down her pants. "Don't you touch me like that again!"

He leaned back against the rail and looked at her. "You've always resented me. Why? What have I done to you?"

"It's what you're doing now. Mother was wrong. The future is not in non-stop expansion."

"You've always had it in for Ma. In fact, the two of us. Yes, you've always resented me. Don't you know I was aware how you poisoned Old Man Shard against me?"

"He made up his own mind. He knew of the cruel things you did."

"How come he didn't know of the cruel things *you* did. Especially to our own mother. She was aware of that. You were always cold to her."

"If I turned cold towards her it was because of the way she reduced a strong man to a weak one. A woman can do that and she knew how. Taking over the running of the ranch from him. All he wanted was a profitable cattle ranch. Not to use the outfit to eat up all the enterprise in the territory.

He was kind, gave her her head, and she made the Circle S unwieldy. It destroyed him. Reduced him to a half man. You won't remember, but she did it to our own father too. I often think that was why he took to an early grave."

"You talk disloyally."

"I talk facts."

"Family members should be loyal to each other."

"Mr Shard and Chris are family. You're not loyal to the one or to the memory of the other."

"They're were never blood kin."

"As good as. To say otherwise is a vile thing." She paused. "Anyway, I came here to warn you. You should be able to see it but you can't. The Circle S will fall apart if you carry on with your hard-headed ways."

"So you came to warn me?" He let the words float on the air then added a loud, dismissive "Huh."

"It's all I can do," she said resignedly, knowing she was hitting her head against a brick wall.

"Ma had got a head for business is all. Same as me."

"That head for business is going to bring the Circle S to its knees."

13

A COUPLE of days on Chris was in town when he heard that a store proprietor had been beaten for refusing to pay the new levy. The trail boss rode hell-for-leather back to the ranch. He found Rufus taking a siesta on the verandah in JJ's old chair, his legs stretched out on another one.

It was clear the noise of Chris's arrival didn't waken him because he remained unmoving until Chris strode up onto the wooden planking and kicked his legs off the chair. The elder brother spluttered into wakefulness with a "What the hell . . . ?"

"Just heard you're still at your old tricks," Chris snapped. "Putting the muscle on the little guy who runs the beer-joint at the end of town. You picked a real tough one there, Brother. Must be at least four foot

135

eleven in his stockinged feet. And fifty years old if he's a day."

"Yeah," Rufus sniggered, "but he's paid his taxes."

Beth came to the door, attracted by the clatter and raised voices.

"Yeah," Chris mimicked. "But it'll take him time to earn it. Talk is he'll be on his back for the best part of a week. Not to mention you and your boys smashing his place up. And just taking what you want out of his cashbox the way you did, that's theft. Straight and simple."

"You never seem to understand, Chris," Rufus said, composing himself. "You gotta show these fellers who's boss. One gets out of line, they'll all follow."

"I've sat and listened to JJ tell you he wanted you to stop that sort of thing."

"And who's he? An old man. An old dead man."

Chris grabbed Rufus's collar, pulling his torso forward. "Don't you bad-talk about him like that in my presence!" As he spoke he let go with one hand and pulled it back in preparation to sledge it into Rufus's face. But there was a click and Chris felt something sharp and hard prod his stomach. The barrel of Rufus's Colt.

Beth saw the development and yelled at them but they were oblivious, remaining in the frozen posture for several seconds, then Chris released his grip and stepped back. "That's the first time you've gone as far as stick a hammered Colt in my gut."

Rufus's features shaped into a leer. "And if you'd tried whupping me that ham fist of yours you'd have found me doing something else with the gun."

Chris repeated his observation. "Yes, that's the first time you've done that."

Rufus smiled. "The way you're going it won't be the last."

"Stop it, you two," Beth yelled. "I can't take it."

More seconds passed with Chris tensed and the Colt levelled; until there came the sound of wheels. Beth glanced at the wagon road and saw an advancing buggy.

"It's Frank," she said. "Put that gun away, Rufus. We don't want to wash our dirty linen in public."

Reluctantly Chris stepped further back. "I'm warning you, Rufus, I'm getting to the end of my tether. Every time I think the Circle S has been dragged as low as it can go, you manage to drag it down another six feet."

Rufus uncocked his gun, and returned it to its holster. "Little brother, I'm warning you too. You see, I enjoy these little donneybrooks we have together. 'Cos I know how they're gonna end one day. Of course, I'll be a little sad, but you won't be getting anything you ain't been asking for for a long time."

"Stop talking like two little kids in a schoolyard," Beth hissed and turned, forcing a smile to greet the visitor.

★ ★ ★

That evening, after Beth and Frank had returned from a buggy ride and Frank had left, Beth went to look at her garden and Chris joined her. After a few words he tried to hold her hand but she pulled away from him. "I'm going to marry Frank."

"What?" Chris couldn't believe his ears.

She repeated the statement.

"But what about us?" he asked in a surprised, cracking falsetto.

"What do you mean — us?"

"I took it for granted, you know, you, me . . . "

"That's one of your troubles, Christopher Shard. You always take things for granted. Why did you think Frank kept on visiting?"

"I thought it was for company."

"Company," she repeated disdainfully and shook her head.

"Where you gonna live?" he asked blankly.

"At Frank's place. Out at the Hourglass."

"But that's miles away."

"Of course it is. That's one of the advantages."

He soughed heavily, still unbelieving. "You love me, don't you?" he said.

She turned away from him and a few seconds passed before she replied. "To be truthful, yes. But it wouldn't work. You and me. Not with the bad feeling between you and Rufus. It would tear me apart, loving both of you and seeing you daily at each other's throats. Like today. You know the whole thing was only a hair's breadth from tragedy? Nearly made me sick. There is going to come a day when the two of you will fight for one last time. Only one of you is going to walk away from that confrontation. That is if you don't kill each other. It's inevitable."

He thought on her words, then spoke slowly. "I'd be a liar if I denied that the thing between me and Rufus will have to come to a head."

"One day it will come. And only one of you will be left standing. One way I lose a brother, the other I lose the man who has my heart." She started crying. "And what of the man remaining. How's he going to feel having killed the other? Whichever one it is." After further sobs: "And how am I going to feel towards him? I can't stay here and watch that happen."

He thought on that, then brightened up. "Beth, let's go away together. Turn our back on the whole shebang. Start afresh somewhere."

She shook her head. "If only it were that easy. Much as I have deep feelings for my brother I know him for what he is: hotheaded, self-interested, short-sighted, cruel. Even more he is a schemer. He would use your going as a pretext for seeing to it that you would lose your inheritance. Mr Shard built this up from nothing, before Ma brought the two of us out here. And he did it for you. When there were only the two of you, him and his little freckle-faced Buster, he wasn't to see that you'd lose two-thirds of what he'd established. If you leave, the way Rufus is, you would leave with nothing."

He drew her towards him. "Hey, if I had to choose between you and my cut of the ranch, I'd choose you."

She pulled away. "I couldn't force you into such a choice."

"You wouldn't be forcing me. So that we could be together, I'd give it all up, freely. You wouldn't be forcing me."

"No, I must go. My staying here forces the choice upon you."

"This is crazy."

"It's reality."

★ ★ ★

The next day Chris was in the tack room cleaning his gear when Rufus came through the door. "You know Beth's leaving to get married?"

"'Course," Chris said, carrying on buffing his saddle. "I'm happy for her." In a sad way, he meant it.

"So am I," Rufus said. "So am I."

142

But the tone was dismissive. "Funny thing is, I always thought you and she might . . . "

Chris didn't respond.

"Huh," Rufus went on reflectively, "suppose I'll have to treat the Hourglass as a special case seeing's it's kinda family. Allow Frank grazing and access to Circle S water. Beth would expect that." But he had more important things to say and his voice firmed up. "Fact is there's implications. Naturally she's retaining her share of the outfit. In her absence she's leaving the management of her share to me. Delegation is the legal term for it. As her blood kin, you understand? Nothing against you personal."

Chris nodded but didn't react.

"That means, dear brother . . . " Rufus paused, and interjected, "dear *step*brother," before he continued, "that means that I have two-thirds share in the running of things. I don't have to justify my decisions to Beth anymore. I am full, unquestioned manager."

Chris nodded again.

"Of course, in the daily run of business I will listen to anything you've got to say," the other went on. "That's only right. We're business partners after all. But, given that you've only got a minority share of the doings, whatever you tell me will legally only have the standing of advice. See, with two-thirds, it's my word that goes. As long as you understand that, we're gonna get along fine. Just like we've always done."

"You and I have got on less and less with the passing of the years. You know that, Rufus."

Rufus shrugged. "We've had our differences but, operating different parts of the outfit, our paths ain't crossed too much. That's suited both of us. You looking after the beef, me looking after boundaries, keeping order about the place. That way we kept out of each other's hair. It can stay like that. Only difference is I make all the top decisions."

There was a heap of questions that went begging in Rufus's statement but Chris moved the discussion to other matters. "You know the old man wanted to change things? Cut down Circle S's interfering in town affairs and business."

"I got some idea of his grumblings. I heard rumours but he never told me his plans direct. Not like you. I didn't have his ear like you did."

"Well, he wanted to get proper law installed, allow the town its freedom, freedom to grow and prosper."

Rufus waved a hand. "The rantings of an old man."

"Don't start that again. I've told you I don't cotton to the way you talk about him."

Rufus raised a placating hand. "OK, but even you'll admit he was getting long in the tooth. However you want to describe it, the point is we can forget all his flapdoodle ideas."

Chris put down his cloth and leant on the saddle. "What about if I don't choose to forget them?"

"I've told you, Chris, you're free to give me all the advice you like. That's what I'm here for. My door is always open. You know that."

"So you're doing nothing about loosening up the town, about selling off our non-cattle interests?"

"We're running a business here, Chris. Ain't sense in selling off lucrative parts of the enterprise."

"So things are gonna go on unchanged?"

"Oh, no, things are gonna change. We don't own all the town. Expansion is still the name of the game. What's the phrase business folk use? Commercially aggressive, that's it. We're gonna be more commercially aggressive."

Chris returned to his task, checking for cracks in the leather of his saddle skirt. "You sure been picking up some high-flown talk from somewheres."

"I been talking to a few folk who know the technicalities of these things if that's what you mean."

"So you don't intend selling off any of the activities?"

Rufus was enjoying himself. He paused, then went on, "Talking about selling off, I'm open to you selling your share of the Circle S to me. I'm in the market. I'll buy it all, hundred cents on the dollar."

"You'd like that, wouldn't you?"

"Like any fair business deal it'd set well with us both. Want me to make you an offer?"

Chris turned on his heel and made for the door. "That'll be the day."

14

THE next day Chris was helping load hay wagons to get fodder out to the herd when Rufus shouted at him from the veranda. "Come and have a look at this."

Chris left his task and returned to the ranch-house.

"What is it?" he asked, entering the study.

Rufus was standing in front of the map on the wall. "You know I don't like taking a large amount of cash out of company funds without keeping you informed," he said, contemplating the map. "Don't want you to think I'm putting my hand in the coffers behind your back. Well, I'm planning to extend the Circle S property to take in the land to the north and east." His hand made a broad sweep over the relevant areas on the map. "What do you think?"

"Don't like it at all."

"Figured not." He turned to his stepbrother with the kind of smile on his face that Chris could have punched. "But I'm telling you in the cause of being nice and friendly. You know, keep you in the picture."

"And what do you want the money for?"

"Gonna take a hell of a lot of barb-wire."

"You know my opinion of barb-wire, Rufus. Rips up cattle and horses. Ours as well as outsiders'. The tradition is free range."

Rufus shrugged. "Well, ain't gonna be free no more," he said and walked over to the safe.

Chris was still studying the map. "What you just marked out, that takes in Dobe Creek. The water there's been accessed by everybody since as far back as I can remember."

"Chris, times are a-changing. It's gonna be wired off. Other outfits wanna use it, they're gonna pay. Top dollar rates too. Worth a fortune to us. Especially in this dry season. They'll be willing to pay anything."

"That's gonna cause more bad feeling."

"There you go again, Chris. We're running a business here. Ain't no room for sentiment in business. Didn't Old Man Shard teach you that?" He took keys from the desk drawer. "So I'm letting you know I'm taking out a thousand for the purchase."

Chris joined him at the safe and watched him take out the money. He knew the argument he would get if he protested any further: Rufus would remind him he voted him down two to one. "How much left?" he asked, as Rufus stuffed the bills into his pocket. He flicked through the remaining money. "Just shy of four grand," he concluded. "Ain't gonna go far at that rate."

★ ★ ★

Chris reached the outskirts of Concho Springs about nine the next morning. He'd had a tiring day previously but he'd got up early to follow up an idea. He avoided the town, guiding his horse towards the white-boarded church on the rise to the south.

He reined in and tied his horse to the hitchrail, clumped up the steps and tried the door. It was locked. Huh, so much for the House of God always being open.

He left his horse where it was and walked the short distance to the clapboard house that he figured was the preacher's home. It was neat, with well-kept flowers and paving up to the door. He banged the knocker and looked back down the main drag while he waited. The sun was still burning the ground rock-hard. Where was the rain?

Sounds came from inside and eventually the door opened to reveal the preacher.

Chris looked from side to side. "Can

we talk, Reverend?"

"Of course we can. Come inside."

In the sitting room the preacher motioned to a chair. "What is this about, my son?"

Chris removed his hat and dropped into the seat. "That matter you came to talk about at the Circle S after the funeral."

"Ah, yes. People are not as God-fearing as they should be. Especially your stepbrother." The voice had taken on the same heavy quality that Chris remembered from the graveside.

"You were quite right to be concerned," Chris continued. "The town, in fact the whole territory, is under the thumb of the Circle S. Let's talk open, Preacher. Like you said, this situation ain't good. For a long time the Circle S has used its muscle to keep new business out. Those businesses it doesn't own it extracts taxes from. It finances the law officer and that means he is at the beck and call of the outfit. Now, none of that is healthy and ain't a basis for founding a thriving community."

"Yes. If you feel this way, isn't there something you can do as an owner of the Circle S?"

"No. My stepbrother is not open to persuasion. Besides, he's got all the control. The matter's got to be tackled another way. There's a need for legitimately elected officials. Like they have in other towns. It would be a step up if the sheriff was a properly elected lawman for a start."

"How do I fit into this?"

"I've come to you because you, more than anyone, should have an interest in seeing that things are set up in a proper manner. What I'm suggesting is, you start pushing folk to organize elections, get folk to run for office."

"I'm not a politician."

"I know, but you got the edge on me in two ways. As a Circle S man I've been cold-shouldered by the community for a long time. I don't know the folk. You'll have a better idea of the right men to handle it, who would do a good job."

"Maybe. What's the other advantage I'm supposed to have?"

"If you try to push 'em to set things up, they'll listen in a way they wouldn't with me. They'd only be suspicious of me as a Circle S man."

The preacher nodded. Then: "But it's you who's initiating the idea for me. How do I know you wouldn't be using me as a cover for some Circle S plan that I can't figure?"

"You don't. Just have to trust me. Anyway, my part in the matter finishes right here and now, if you say you'll take some action. I'll have nothing to do with candidates or the elections, except for casting my vote like any other citizen."

"I don't understand what you're getting out of it. Surely the Circle S has a lot to lose by letting go its grip on the law office and the rest of the town."

"In the short term yes, but in the long term the town should prosper and that benefits everybody, the Circle S included."

"Forgive me. These are wise words, not the kind you expect to hear coming from the lips of one so young."

"You put a man into the ground not long ago. You've only been here a short while so you won't have known him and I won't blame you for judging him by the poor attendance at his funeral. You will have heard bad talk against him. It wasn't justified. He was a good man. He founded the Circle S with only hard work and fair trading in mind. But the outfit took a bad turn some years back. He allowed control to be taken by his wife. She was a ruthless empire builder and the Circle S got a bad name. Even when she died he hadn't realized how bad a name his business had developed. But, somehow, he recently came to learn of the way local folk saw the outfit and he was intent on changing things. However, his fatal accident put an end to all that."

"Yes, I'm a young man, you're right. Still got fuzz on my chin. But I would like to see an old man's ideas put into practice. For my part I'm going to do everything I can to see to it that the Circle S divests itself of its non-cattle businesses. That'll open up the town to healthy competition. I aim to open negotiations with neighbouring spreads so that we can live amicably side by side. I'll admit, scaling down the Circle S operation is not going to be easy. I share the ownership with my stepbrother Rufus and he's as hard-nosed as his mother. But I think in time I might be able to swing it, especially if democracy starts to get a hold. The way I see it, if the town loosens up, he should start to see sense and allow the Circle S to loosen up too."

He readjusted himself in the chair by way of emphasis. "What I would like you to do is set the ball rolling in town so that it moves towards a democratic community in the American way."

The preacher had been watching his eyes; figured he detected honesty. "That's a fine speech, son. I think you mean it. You leave it with me. I do know of some good men. We'll see if we can get elections organized."

15

CHRIS stood at the back, hymn-book in hand, singing as loud as the rest of them. He'd never had much time for church-going — cattle didn't recognize Sunday — but he'd made time this week. He was eager to know how the election business was going. He listened to the sermon, sang another hymn then waited at the door while the preacher shook the hands of the departing congregation.

"Make any progress on the matter we discussed?" he asked, after the last parishioner had bidden goodbye.

"Indeed," the preacher said. "An *ad hoc* committee has been set up. Even given me an *ex officio* position on it. The thing's led by Stacy Magee. You know him?"

"The dry-goods store man?"

"Yes. They plan to hold two elections.

One for sheriff and one for the town council. They aim for six members of council and the elected councillors will then select the mayor from their number."

"Seems workable. Who's running?"

The preacher went through the names of the committee and a couple of others who had been nominated. Chris nodded. Some he knew, some he didn't. "And who's running for sheriff?"

"Only two. Ruddock, the incumbent and a fellow called Dee Pascal. You know him?"

"No. Any qualifications for the job?"

"Rides shotgun for the stage-line. Did a spell on guard duty at the court in Austin one time. Only temporary when they were short-staffed. That counts for something, I suppose."

Chris smiled. "In Concho Springs that's the equivalent of a Harvard law degree."

"The closing day for nominations is tomorrow, so the posters should be up early in the week."

Chris stepped out onto the porch and set his hat on his head. "This is working out smoother than I expected." He put out his hand. "Thanks, Reverend."

★ ★ ★

The stagedriver pulled on the handbrake as his shotgun rider dropped down. "See you, Dee."

Dee Pascal returned his companion's farewell and headed along the boardwalk, his shotgun canted over his arm. He paused at the end of town and looked at the poster on the last building. He'd never seen his name in letters like that; and underneath, the exhortation to vote for him as sheriff of Concho Springs. He savoured it. Sheriff of Concho Springs . . . that would be something.

He'd been shotgun rider for the stage-line for almost a year but it kept him away from home for long nights at a stretch and his missus kept pressing him to get a job in town.

However, until the sheriff's job came up there'd been nothing. Of course it was not a dead cert but there was a good chance he would stack enough votes to get it. He was well liked in town. Physically he was suitable, being strongly built. His background was appropriate: riding shotgun he was seen as a capable man. Moreover he had once carried a gun for money as court guard in Austin. Wasn't much — it hadn't lasted long — but it sounded good. But, just as important, he only had one rival for the position, Ruddock. And the committee were pretty sure the incumbent wouldn't get many votes because he was a Circle S man.

Insects spun busily in the twilight as he strode out of town. He and his missus had got this small homestead a short way out of town: chickens for eggs, a goat for milk and a vegetable patch. That worried him at the moment; it needed water and there hadn't been rain for quite spell now. And the well was running low.

He whistled softly as he walked, thinking of his missus and the apple pie that awaited him.

He was well clear of the town when his reverie was shattered by a man suddenly stepping out from behind a boulder in front of him. Even in the fading light he recognized the man. From the Circle S. He knew his name, Rufus, and he knew that he didn't like him.

"Howdy, neighbour," the stageman said, coming to a standstill.

The other ignored his greeting. "So you're the one aiming to be the new sheriff, eh?"

Dee looked around. The man seemed to be alone. "I'm running for the office if that's what you mean. Say, what's this all about?"

"Seems to me a man running for such a post needs to be handy with a gun."

"I can handle them."

"Oh yeah, you've toted a gun. But

toting a gun and having experience using it in a working situation are two different things."

"Listen, it's late. I've had a long day. I've got a home and a meal to go to. So if you don't mind."

He made to continue on his way but was halted by Rufus sidestepping and blocking his path.

"I ain't got time for foolery," Dee said impatiently.

"This ain't foolery, mister. See, as a citizen and voter I got a right to know what a candidate's qualifications are for a public office like lawman. For instance, have you ever killed a man?"

"No."

"So you don't know how you'd act if that was something the job required you to think about?"

"I think I could do it if I had to. Like a man might shoot a rabid dog. It ain't something you think about, you just do it. But one hopes the situation doesn't arise."

"See, your answer was OK till that last statement. You let yourself down. It betrays a softness. The job requires a man to be hard."

"Concho Springs ain't Tombstone or Deadwood."

Rufus maintained his stony gaze on the other's eyes. "Could be. A man choosing to pack a star must be ready for all eventualities. Why, even here a lawman could face a guy who wants to put some lead into him. You ever faced a man who's out to kill you?"

"No, but this is all hypothetical."

"We're talking the same language again. That's why I want to get down to practicalities. Here and now."

The blood drained from Dee's face. He shifted uncomfortably. "Listen, I don't want any trouble. See." He lowered his shotgun to the ground.

A grin broadened Rufus's face. "Now you're getting the right idea. I want to see how well you can use your side iron."

Dee moved slightly. Whether he was

going for his gun, in fact he wasn't, was immaterial. The movement was enough cause for Rufus; and his hand blurred. There was a bang and the shotgun rider was lying on his back with a hole in his chest.

Rufus moved forward, looked down and checked him over for vital signs. The fellow was an ex-shotgun rider.

"Mount up, boys," Rufus said. "Back to town for the last phase of tonight's operation."

* * *

There were still a few men in Concho Springs who were untainted by the Circle S. There were those who couldn't be touched by the outfit's chicanery by the very nature of their activities. The operator and his assistant in the Telegraph and Mail Office. They were employees of the US Government. So that was one establishment the Circle S couldn't take over or extract taxes from. Similarly untouchable were

165

those who worked for big out-of-town companies, such as the manager of the bank.

Even the Circle S didn't dare risk incurring the wrath of powerful outside companies.

Then there was a handful of men who were independent simply through strength of character: Doc Crane, for one. And another was Stacy Magee who ran the general store. Thus it was that there were men prepared to organize or run for public office in the face of the Circle S monopoly.

At the moment Magee was working late in his store bringing his accounts up to date. With blinds drawn he didn't see four riders come in from the flats.

The three pulled up at a saloon and hitched their horses.

"This one must be handled a little more quietly," the leader said as the three gathered before the boardwalk. "A gunshot miles out on the flats ain't gonna be heard but in town we gotta be a mite more subtle. We'll take a drink, relax a spell then slip out the back, leaving Spike in the saloon for some cover."

A quarter-hour later they were walking along the alley that ran at the back of the buildings. They stopped at the lighted window at the back of Magee's store.

Rufus took out his gun and knocked the door.

"We're closed," came Magee's voice.

"I know," Rufus said with his mouth close to the crack between door and jamb, "but I'd like to place an order for supplies."

"Can't it wait till morning?"

"Well, I just happen to be riding through town back to my place. It's a big order and I was thinking if I give you the list now you can get it ready and packed up, so save time when I come back tomorrow."

"Very well." There was the sound of feet on boards, then a key turning.

As the door opened Rufus pushed his way through followed by his sidekicks.

Before Magee could voice his surprise Rufus slammed him across the head with his gun butt.

With the door closed Rufus looked down for a second time that evening at a downed man. "He's out," he concluded.

He scanned the room. The table on which Magee had been working was laden with figured paper, neat piles of coins and bills and a flickering oil-lamp. He pointed to two unlit lamps on the walls. "Get me them and find where he keeps the oil."

Arnie crossed to one of the lamps while Moses went in search of the fuel. As they set about their tasks Magee groaned some more and gave signs of coming to. "Hurry up, you two," Rufus grunted and whammed the storeman again with his gun butt.

As the leader emptied the two lamps over the room Moses located a can in a cupboard. Rufus took it, unscrewed the cap and utterly doused the fallen Magee, making sure his whole shape was covered with the liquid.

He took the burning lamp from the desk and backed from the scene. "OK, boys, outside." When his companions were clear he took the key from the lock then slung the lamp on the unconscious form. He waited long enough to see man was enveloped with flame, then shot outside and locked the door, slinging the key.

"What happens if he lives?" Moses wanted to know.

Rufus sniggered. "Huh, there's no way he'll live through that. Now back to the saloon and take it easy. We'll rejoin Spike like nothing's happened."

16

AS Chris drew up to the white fence marking the entrance to the church he could see proud parents with a baby emerging from the building following a christening. He dismounted and kept his distance as the party of smiling relatives and friends made its way down the path.

While he waited he tweaked his shirt front to get air to his sweating torso. Much more of this waterless heat and there would be cattle dying.

At the gate the preacher gave his final blessings and Chris bided his time until the group had departed. Then he said, "I guess you know why I've come."

The preacher looked at him and nodded, drawn features replacing his professional baptism smile. "Guess so. Ghastly business. I was utterly sickened when I learned."

"Anyone know the culprits?"

"No. Pascal's killing was attributed to some unknown thief and Magee's death is being claimed as an accident." He looked heavenward. "I feel so culpable, initiating their involvement in the wretched affair."

"How do you think I feel? It was me who mooted the idea in the first place."

The preacher put his hand on Chris's arm "No, don't feel that. I was as much a party to it as you were. And they entered into the election of their own free will."

"No, Father. It was my fault. I was acting like a greenhorn. I should have known it wasn't going to be that easy. Trouble is, you make a mistake and somebody else pays the price."

"Well, one thing's for sure: it marks the end of any liberalization ideas in Concho Springs. The remaining men have withdrawn their nominations and the election arrangements have collapsed. Everybody's as scared as rabbits."

"Figure that was the intention."

The preacher let out a sigh. "Now I have the invidious task of saying the last rites over the poor men." He looked at the now distant parents with their white-swathed bundle. "One compensation afforded by my line of work is at least I see children begin their way in the world."

Chris began to untie the knot of his reins. "Yes, but what kind of a world is it going to be?"

* * *

Riding into town, Chris dismounted close to what was left of Magee's general store and tied his horse to a rail across the street. He walked over and surveyed the blackened, burnt-out shell. No chance of any kind of clues there.

He walked further into town, pushed open the law office door and heavy-footed in. Ruddock was at the stove preparing coffee and he looked up to see what kind of visitor didn't knock or wait for an invitation. He held rein on his intended rebuke and pointed to the coffee pot. "Oh. Howdy, Chris. Want some?"

"Ain't come for socializing. Want to know what you got on the two killings and what you're doing about 'em."

"Hold on there, Chris. One was a killing for sure. Doc found a slug in Pascal. But the other has all the signs of an accident. Looks like Magee had had a busy day and fell asleep at his desk, knocking a lamp over."

"Happening the same evening, you don't think the two are connected?"

"Coincidence."

"And I suppose it's a coincidence again that both the victims were running for the new elections."

"I'd say so. Pity about that."

"Yeah, I reckon you're real sorry." He watched the lawman take a sip of coffee, then asked, "You been out to where Pascal got it?"

"Yeah. No useful sign. Ground's baked hard, there being no rain for so long."

"Anybody seen any strangers about, in town or riding through?"

"No."

"What kind of slug did the Doc take out of him?"

"Forty-five."

Rufus toted a .45, a fact Chris almost mentioned, just stopping himself when he realized anything he dropped out in front of Ruddock would go straight back to his stepbrother. Instead, he said, "Well, that's one kind of clue, ain't it? Can't you work on that?"

Ruddock laughed drily. "Almost every man with a side iron has a forty-five." He gestured towards Chris's hand weapon. "Even you. No, that don't help none."

"What's my brother got to say about all this?"

"He's been very concerned. Even offered his boys as a posse if I get any angles and need some back-up."

"Very public spirited of him." With that he stepped outside once again.

★ ★ ★

Back at the ranch Rufus was waiting for him in the study. "Where you been?" he asked, as Chris slung his hat onto a chair and dropped wearily into another.

"Finding out about Pascal and Magee." He studied his brother, looking for something in his face as he said the words. Seeing nothing, he went on, "Their deaths are sure convenient for the Circle S. At least, for your way of running the Circle S."

"What's that supposed to mean?"

"Rufus you're a cold fish. And a hard one. You'd have no compunction to eliminate somebody who stands in your way."

"Now that ain't brotherly talk."

"It's because I'm your brother that I know what you're capable of. And it's because I'm your brother I can say it."

He paused, then asked, "Where were you and the boys last night?"

"In town as usual. So were lots of folk. Listen, Chris, I don't know what you're insinuating but you got no call to talk this way." He stood up and dropped his backside on the desk top. "I told you I'm a mite concerned about law and order going downhill. More folks causing us trouble around the borders of the spread. It's got the look of a general trend, as more outsiders move into the territory. The events of last night confirm it. You remember I was looking to take on a few more guns, well, I'm aiming to do that now. I've told Ruddock I can loan him Circle S men as deputies if he needs them. Now more men'll need cash, you understand, so I'm just letting you know I'm gonna be taking some more funds. Like I've told you, I don't need your permission: I'm just telling you friendly-like as it's company money."

He walked to the safe and worked

the combination. Chris joined him and looked over his shoulder as he delved into the contents.

"While you've got it open there's my men to pay too," he said. He took out a wad and entered the amount in a cash book, handing the pencil to his brother to record his withdrawal.

He stuffed the bills in his pocket, picked up his hat and walked to the door. "Thought I'd take some for legitimate expenses — while there's still some left in the piggy bank."

17

"**I**'ll see to your horse for you," Cy offered, noting Chris's tiredness. "You get yourself into the shade with some of your Aunt Mary's lemonade."

Chris had just returned from three bone-wearying days on the range. Getting fodder out to the scattered herd was becoming a problem. "Thanks, Cy," he said and swung down passing over the reins.

"'Fraid you've come back to bad news, Chris," the old-timer said as he began uncinching the saddle. "Somebody's knocked over the outfit's safe."

"When? How?"

Cy was about to explain when Rufus's voice boomed from a distance. "Howdy, Chris." He turned to see his brother coming from the bunkhouse.

Cy let the saddle fall to ground. "Rufus'll tell you," he said and turned his attention to slipping off the bridle.

Chris watched him turn the horse loose in the corral while he waited for his brother to reach him. "What's this about the safe?" he asked, when the man was close.

"Ah, Cy's told you? Yeah. Cleared it out."

"Who?"

"Dunno. Some sneaky varmint."

"How come?"

"Yesterday morning. In the early hours."

"Who else knew the combination?"

"Didn't need to. Used explosive."

Chris gave a disgusted whistle. "Who'd be crazy enough to do something like that? Explosive? They'd have the boys on 'em before they could get clear of the place."

"No boys about. You and your lot were up at the line camp. Me and mine were staying over in town. And you know the Mexes, sleep through anything. Cy and his missus were fast asleep too. Took them some time to find out what had happened by which time whoever it was had got clean away."

"Let's have a look," Chris said, stepping up quickly into the building. He made his way to the study to find the safe standing forlorn, open and empty.

He walked around it, touching it, inspecting it. "Anything to go on?"

"The old folk thought they heard a horse or horses afterwards, but that's all. There was no moon and they couldn't see anything."

"Headed which way?"

"They couldn't be sure. You know the way sound carries at night."

"Well, one thing's for sure. Whoever it was knew something about the place. Knew there was something worth stealing and where it was. Knew their way around. And knew both sets of men were away."

"That's what I was thinking. An

180

inside job, mebbe. Any of your boys gone missing?"

"Hell, no," Chris snapped. "What about yours?"

"Leave mine out of it. I can account for all of 'em."

"Has Ruddock been out here?"

"No point. Of course I reported it to him but he knows less than we do."

Chris drummed his fingers on the desk. "Hell, that's all our hard cash, Rufus. How we gonna pay the men?"

"There's the account in town."

Chris opened up the ledger. "According to the book there was over five thousand in there."

"Yeah, some haul. And they say crime doesn't pay."

Chris dropped into a chair and ran his teeth over his thumbnail. "Rufus, this is one hell of a blow."

"You don't have to tell me."

"We're gonna have to pull in our belts. Time to think about letting some of the men go."

"We'll get by. I'm certainly not giving

any of my crew the burlap. I've got a loyal bunch. I ain't rewarding loyalty with a handshake. If we're gonna have to let men go it'll have to be some of the cowmen. Their payroll is our biggest labour cost, anyhows."

"Of course they constitute our biggest labour cost, we're running a beef outfit. Hell, can't shave the cow crew. They're overworked as it is."

They sat in silence for a while. Chris smelt a rat but said nothing. For a start Rufus didn't seem as disturbed as he should have been.

* * *

Chris and Deuce were swinging across the range looking for strays. With no rain to break the relentless sun, grass was getting sparse and cows were straying further afield. They were picking their way through a straggle of chaparral approaching Dobe Creek when Deuce reined in and pointed to a stand of cottonwoods on a ridge to their side. "What the hell's that?"

Chris brought his mount to halt and squinted in the indicated direction. Plainly silhouetted against the sky two shapes were hanging from the branches. "Jesus, there's been a lynching."

They spurred their horses up the shallow grade, slowing as they neared the scene. One corpse was still and the other turned slightly, the branch above it creeking eerily.

It wasn't the first time Chris had seen a dead man, but the sight was still stomach-churning. "If I ain't mistaken this is more of Rufus's doing," Chris muttered, as he studied the sad countenances. Signs were they'd been there some days.

He walked over the ridge and looked down the slant of the other side. There were dead cows near the water-hole.

"Looks like there's been some kind of a ruckus here," he said on his return. "Rufus was on about stopping other outfits using the water here. I told him Dobe Creek's always been open access."

With faces tight from the smell and the general unpleasantness of the task they cut the bodies down and laid them side by side at the bole of a tree. Chris went through the pockets but there was nothing to serve as identification. "This would be a job for the law if we had any. As it is, all we can do is the decent thing. Ride back to the camp. Get a shovel and a couple of volunteers to help you bury 'em. I'll go back to the casa and find out what this is all about."

★ ★ ★

Chris banged open the bunkhouse door. Rufus was playing cards with his sidekicks.

"Just been cleaning up after your dirty work," Chris snapped, standing in the still open doorway.

Rufus folded his hand. "What's the problem, Brother?"

"Earlier on today, cut down a couple of waddies that had been strung up at Dobe Creek."

"Shouldn't have done that. They were left as a warning." He grinned and looked round the faces of his companions. "You know, like you nail a dead fox to the fence near a chicken run."

"We're talking about human beings, not playing games. All they seem to have done was broke through some barb-wire to get their cattle to water."

"That was enough."

"You know my opinion on barb-wire."

"They were trespassing. They damaged company property, used Circle S facilities without permission. We gave 'em due warning, didn't we, boys?"

"Like hell you did."

"These bozos have gotta know we mean business. Listen, I don't tell you how to run the cows, you don't tell me how to police the range. That's the arrangement."

"If you wanna frighten trespassers off, pepper a few holes in the sky if you have to. You don't have to murder 'em."

Rufus turned back to his cards. "You was allus the soft one, Chris."

"The civilized one, you mean. Well, with no law, there's no one to bring you to book. But it ain't always gonna be like that."

18

RUFUS was getting more cold-blooded He'd enjoyed killing the trespassers. He was turning the place into its own little hell on earth. At the same time, the way he was burning up the assets he would bleed the Circle S dry. The only spendable dough remaining was in the bank account. On paper neither owner could touch it without the say-so of the other. In reality, it was a sure bet Rufus would find a way of swinging it with his lawyer friend to make whatever withdrawals from it he chose. Probably to the point of cleaning it out. As he had the safe. Equally sure was that he would stymie any attempt by Chris to make withdrawals in the same way.

Hell, what should he do? Things were getting worse. Beth had been right and wrong at the same time.

Leaving the place, going with her, would have meant giving up his stake, or at least a fair chunk of it. With Chris permanently out of the way, Rufus would stumble on some device to reduce his stepbrother's claim. Chris could live with that if it was the necessary price he had to pay to be with Beth. But what he couldn't have lived with was leaving something that had taken his old man a lifetime to build up; leaving it to a wastrel like Rufus.

OK, so he had stayed on. So what? What good was that doing? Just increasing his frustration, that's what.

He lit a smoke and thought the thing round in circles. There had to be some way of getting a grip on the Circle S and straightening it out. It was like a maverick bull steer, thundering along under its own impetus, heading for some deep ravine, unseen but nevertheless there. But there were ways of stopping a wayward hunk of beef. He was a cowman, he knew that.

There should be a way of stopping the downward spiral of the Shard outfit.

Thoughts began to coalesce. Rufus's power depended on his gang of gunnies. To keep them he needed to pay them. His ability to pay depended on the prosperity of the Circle S. That was it. If Chris could devise some way to bring the Circle S down; not to ruin it, that would defeat the object, but bring it down sufficiently for Rufus to be stuck for ready dollars. That way his stepbrother would find that the loyalty of his sidekicks was only as deep as his pocket.

How could he work it? Rufus held all the aces.

But did he? Not quite. There was the remainder of the stock. That had value; it was scattered wide over the Circle S land but it was an asset that Chris could liquidate. The more he thought about it the more he saw that as his next step. What he should do beyond that was another matter. But first things first. How could he round up the steers and head them up to Abilene without Rufus knowing? He and his henchmen could ride faster than a moving herd. One whiff of Chris's plan and he could catch up and confront Chris; maybe ride with Chris to Abilene to make sure he got his share of the proceeds; and there were always his gunnies to settle any dispute.

So if he was to do it, it had to be done on the quiet. A crew moving a herd needed several kinds of back-up. A wagon-load of food for starters. Then miscellaneous supplies: spare clothing to replace damaged ones; straps, thongs, and all the little things necessary for running repairs on the drive: all the bits and pieces to tackle the unanticipated snags like broken cinches, snapped reins, broken wheels. And finally a remuda of replacement horses. A drover changed horses at least once a day when on the move. There was no way Chris could take the outfit's horses without raising his brother's suspicions. That was out of the question. The crew would have to make do with their existing mounts and maybe Chris could put some kind of remuda together by buying horses on the way. It was unlikely he could get hold of a full set of replacements, but maybe enough to get by.

However, supplies constituted the first major problem. If Rufus heard that Chris had headed out with a fully-laden supply wagon he would put two and two together. If Chris was to leave the Circle S with a wagon, he needed a cover.

He was thinking on these things with a silent Deuce at his side when a puncher rode in from the line camp. Chris watched him unsaddle his horse and haze it into the corral.

They exchanged greetings and the fellow relayed the news that everything was OK at the line camp.

Mrs McKinney cooked up some chow for the hungry cowman and Chris along with Deuce sat with him while he ate. Then Chris remembered there'd been another cow fever scare. He questioned the man on the matter.

"No problem, Chris. False alarm. All we saw of the passing herd was dust. There's been no contact between the two stocks."

Chris thought on it, then said, "Don't tell anyone the suspect herd has moved on." They were alone and he knew he could trust the pair of them so he explained the idea that had come to him: his intention of rounding up the herd and driving it up to Abilene. "It's got to be under wraps," he said. "Rufus is not to know. So, we need a reason for taking a stocked-up supply wagon. I'll tell him the cow fever still presents a risk and we need to move the steers. We'll need extra supplies for that. That way Rufus shouldn't be suspicious when we head out with a full wagon."

★ ★ ★

"They say trouble comes in threes," he said. "First there was the thieving of our money. I don't know what number three is, but number two is the threat of cow fever. You remember we got news of a passing herd with diseased steers? Well, they coasted past without incident but one of my crew's ridden in to tell me there's another one. Bigger herd this time. More chance of contagion. This time we gotta shift our steers clear and pronto."

Rufus nodded, uninterestedly.

Chris took a chance. "Like to loan me some of your men. We're gonna need every hand we can get. Ain't exactly a minor operation." The last thing he wanted was any of Rufus's men watching what was going on, but he banked on Rufus declining. He was right.

"My men are pistoleers. They wouldn't know one end of a cow from another." He chuckled. "Besides, they wouldn't thank me for volunteering 'em."

Chris figured his offer to take some of Rufus's rotten apples on board would legitimize the operation in his brother's eyes, and it had.

"No," Rufus concluded. "I'm sure you can handle it, Chris."

"OK, I'll head out in the morning. Like I said, it'll be a big operation so you won't see me for the best part of a week."

"Take as long as you like."

★ ★ ★

Chris left the ranch the next day. His tale about shifting cows due to the threat of cow-fever worked so he left without raising Rufus's suspicions, despite riding out with a fully-loaded supply wagon, the complement of horses from the corral and the remainder of the Mexicans who normally stayed on at the ranch for fence-mending and other chores.

He'd only got one regret: that he had not been able to see Beth before he had departed. She had been spending more and more time at Turner's ranch, he felt sure just to be away from the Circle S, so it had been no surprise that she was not around when he'd hit the trail.

When he reached the line camp he explained his plan and the following day the tedious routine of round-up began. It took the best part of a week to hunt out the scattered grazers, burn the Circle S brand on the flank of unmarked mavericks they'd picked up and herd the lot into a box canyon.

Late one afternoon, when he figured the first phase of the operation was over, he took a walk to an elevated point and looked down. Using a tally string, moving his fingers from knot to knot each time he counted a hundred, it was with some satisfaction that he estimated nigh on a thousand.

Returning to the camp he gave the order and the following morning they pointed the beeves north.

They drove the steers hard for the

first week in order to get them off familiar range as fast as possible. Cows weren't a hundred per cent stupid and would return to home territory given half a chance. Also it took time to trail-break a herd so it was policy to keep them whacked out at the beginning so they were too tired to think of running at sundown. Until they got into the routine of things.

Trail driving was a dangerous occupation, hot, dry and dusty to boot. It took know-how and stamina but Chris had got a trail crew that he could rely on. They could handle it.

He could handle it too, having accompanied his stepfather on drives to Abilene since he was first out of knee-britches. He knew where good water was to be had, even in these dry times, the tried and tested places for bedding down the cattle, and the safest points for river crossings. No problem; the trail was worked into his blood and bones.

19

THEY made Abilene without hitch. Chris gave the order to bed down the herd some miles out while he rode ahead to clear delivery. It was getting dark when he reached the railhead but he knew his way about, knew who to see. Establishing that there were vacant holding pens he returned to the herd to tell the men to prepare for a move-out at sun-up.

* * *

"It's a deal." Hands were clenched and the two men turned to lean on the fence and look at the merchandise.

The two men couldn't have looked more unalike. The Circle S trail boss was filmed in dust head to toe; the other, Jed Stevens, cattle

197

buyer, immaculate in suit and derby. "Always a pleasure doing business with you, Chris," Stevens said after he had written out a bank draft for the requisite amount.

"Likewise, Jed," Chris rejoined, checking the draft before slipping it into his wallet.

Jed Stevens had set up stall in Abilene not long after its founding as a railhead and had had dealings with the elder Shard from the early days.

"Real sorry to hear about your pa," he added. "Was always a pleasure doing business with him too. The two of you always ran a square outfit, supplied prime beef, no trouble with documents and tallies." He paused, then asked, "How exactly did it happen?"

Chris related the circumstances of his step-father's death. "There might have been a touch of providence about it," he concluded. "It wasn't until after his death that I learned he had been seriously ill."

"Kept it to himself, did he?"

"Yeah."

"That'd be old stoic JJ." He ruminated on it then took a pack from his pocket. "Fancy a store-made cigarette?"

Chris took one.

"You aiming to carry on the business?" Stevens asked after they had lighted up.

"Funny you should ask that. I'm hankering to take a break. Your offer for a post as buyer — that still open?"

"Sure. I'd be grateful to have you but what about the Circle S?"

"Well, ownership is shared by three of us. You won't know my stepbrother and sister."

"No, but your old man talked of them of course. Belonged to his wife from a former marriage?"

"Yeah. Anyway, situation's complicated and I don't want to say anymore than that, but I got a yen for a change of scenery. Just to get the place outa my hair for a spell. Give me time to think. Taking up your offer would fit the bill."

"Sure thing, Chris. If it'd be a help to you, it'd be a help to me."

Chris felt some unease. He'd never been content to take another man's wage; the notion of being under somebody's else's thumb for his weekly dollars didn't set too well in his head. "Snag is," he went on, "don't know how long for."

"Don't matter. Even if it's just for a few weeks, it'd be a service. Can't trust nobody in this cut-throat business. I get knifed every time I put trust in a guy." He thought on it. "Say, this has fell good. I need to get back East for a spell to talk with the men in the grey suits. I've knowed your old man for fourteen years, and knowed you since he first brung you up here forking a cow pony. You and he are two of a kind. I can trust you. And that's what I need: somebody who knows cattle and ain't gonna be playing with another deck when my back's turned. How does fifteen dollars a week sound?"

Chris waggled his head, then said,

"Twenty including accommodation and found?"

"You strike a hard bargain."

"I thought you wanted somebody who could dicker?"

Stevens chuckled and they shook hands again.

★ ★ ★

A quarter-hour later Chris stepped out of the bank where he had cashed the draft and he headed back to the holding pens. The Circle S men were congregated beside a windmill that spilled water into a catch tank alongside a pen. Calling them together Chris took out his tally book and pencil which he handed to Deuce, then took out his bulging wallet. "Seeing's this is a parting, I'm giving you all a bonus," he announced.

For each crewmember Deuce stated the man's due according to his station. Chris counted the amount, then added a big bill to each. The longer serving men shook Chris's hand.

"I don't need to tell you," Chris said, when each man had signed and taken receipt, "the Circle S has no stock now. So it don't need a cow crew at the moment. I don't know how things are panning out but Rufus might aim to build up a new herd. If that's the case there could be work with the outfit if you're at a loose end and choose to ride back there."

"I ain't at that much of a loose end," one man said loudly. His comment was trailed by similar statements around the gathering. On that matter the men were of one mind: they didn't cotton to working for the Circle S without Chris, and certainly not if it meant working for Rufus.

As the rumbling died down one herder held up his take as though it was a trophy in some race. "You'll honour me, Mr Shard, if you accompany me to the nearest liquor parlour where I can drink to your good health."

Chris smiled in appreciation and

gestured down the front of his dusty garb. "I got time to wash and shave first?"

There was a chorus of "No" as he was hoisted aloft by the nearest crewmembers and the whole bunch headed for the saloon.

20

THREE months passed. The Circle S men had long since gone their separate ways and Chris had settled into his new occupation.

Jed Stevens had journeyed East several times, happy to leave his cattle buying to Chris. The former trail boss was living a comfortable life but he was restless. It was too comfortable. Town life didn't suit him. He missed the wind in his hair, the feel of a saddle under him. He smoked too much and ate richly without hard physical exercise to work off the fat. With empty evenings to fill he pulled too many corks too; not enough to get loop-legged but enough to add even more inches to his midsection.

He wondered how the Circle S was doing, how Mrs McKinney was coping.

He'd felt real bad about leaving the old lady, like he'd deserted her. But he'd sent her a note explaining, and hoped she'd understand. He hankered to know how the outfit was faring. Had Rufus got in a new crew? Was he building up a new herd?

He itched to know of these things but he was too proud to make enquiries. Rufus would have long realized he had cut away; and would be content for his stepbrother to fry in his own fat.

More than anything Chris missed Beth. The big blow came when he learned from a passing drover that she'd married. A big chunk of that was his own fault. She'd always been reserved with him and he'd respected that, holding back from her. That funny sister/brother thing had always got in the way of both of them for as long as he could remember and for that reason he'd always held back from her. Of course, he was expecting it. She'd stated her intention but the news still sent him on a jag, rare for him, for a couple of days. When he came out of it he reconciled himself with the view that she had staked out her own life and that was that. He just hoped she was happy, was all. But he still had pangs of envy when he thought about her husband.

However, his job was going fine, having just concluded another satisfactory purchase for Stevens and he was taking a celebratory drink in an Abilene saloon with the seller, when he heard a familiar voice. "Hi there, Mr Shard."

He turned to see Rufus's sidekick, Spike. Without a smile, Chris just said the man's name in acknowledgement.

Spike sashayed up close. "Can we have a parley in private, Mr Shard?" he went on with a deference in his voice Chris had never heard before.

Chris looked at his business companion. "Excuse me, sir." He rose and followed the Circle S man to a quiet section of the bar.

"You're a long ways from home,

Spike. What is it?"

"Thing is, Mr Shard, Rufus wants to know if you'll come back."

Chris showed no reaction. "That's a new shake of the dice. What for?"

"Things are running bad at the Circle S."

"He's supposed to be the manager. Didn't he take on a new crew, get a new herd together?"

Spike laughed. "There's no money left. What he didn't drink and spend on hoorah girls he gambled away."

"So there's no new stock?"

"No. Ain't got the scratch for it."

"What about the so-called taxes he bleeds out of Concho Springs?"

"Down to a dribble. He ain't got no strongarm boys to back it up."

"What about Arnie, Moses and the others?"

"They've all seen the writing on the wall and vamoosed. There's only me left. Fact is, the boss'd sure like you to come back. Says he's sorry for the way he's treated you."

"Huh, I'd have to hear that from him."

"You ride back and you will. He's handing you the reins. The place is falling apart round his ears. You're the only one to get the outfit back on its feet."

"He said that, did he?"

"Yeah."

"And what are the strings?"

"No strings."

Chris thought on it. His plan had worked, and quicker than he'd expected. He'd had mixed feelings about cutting loose. He'd told himself it was for the best but deep down he felt he had taken a coward's way out. Now he was vindicated. He just hoped there was enough left of the Circle S to put back together again.

★ ★ ★

The windows of the ranch were dirty.

When Chris had crossed the northern boundary he had been increasingly aware of the absence of cattle. Then, to ride for three hours into the heart of Shard territory without hearing the lowing of steers had been danged eerie. Even weirder was the lack of bustle as he had ridden under the arch and approached the ranch-house. Not a soul. Like some ghost ranch.

But what really told Chris that things were rock bottom was the grimy windows of the house itself. Strange, how clean windows were a barometer of the health of a place. In the fourteen years that Chris had lived there, not a week had gone by without Mrs McKinney or her man buffing up the glass like it was top-dollar crystal. Even old man Shard had commented on it more than once. Must have had something to do with the ancient housekeeper's puritan upbringing; cleanliness is next to Godliness. Well, either something had happened to the old lady — which he hoped not — or God was no longer in residence at the Shard hacienda.

It certainly wasn't God who came to the door, drawn by the sound of Chris's arrival. It was Rufus.

"Howdy, Brother."

Chris ignored the greeting. "How's Mrs McKinney?"

"OK, why?"

Chris was glad to hear so. And the reply had told him why the windows were dirty. The old gal had as much interest in pulling out the stops for the ornery Rufus as the crewmembers he'd left back in Abilene.

He stepped up onto the veranda and pulled off his riding gloves. "Spike says you asked for me?"

"Yeah, yeah. Come on in. You must be trail weary. Rest your bones. I'll get you a drink."

The study was a mess, a condition that Shard would never have tolerated: dust, garbage, empty bottles and soiled plates.

"Well, what's it all about?" Chris asked, when he was settled in a chair with a glass of cheap corn.

"All is forgiven," Rufus said, forcing a smile.

"What the hell is there to forgive?"

"Riding off with what was left of the herd like you did. And all the other stuff between us."

Chris restricted his comment on Rufus's warped angle of looking at things to a hard grunt. "So?"

"Didn't Spike tell you?"

"I wanna hear it from you."

"Chris, the old place is turning into a festering sore. We're near bust. I know you ain't bothered about me but if the outfit folds we all lose. You and Beth as well as me. And you're the only one who can pull the thing out of it."

Chris let the notion hang in the air for a spell. This was what he'd been waiting for. "Gotta be on my terms," he said. "A free hand. A completely free hand."

"Understood."

Chris proffered his empty glass and nodded to the bottle for a top-up. Rufus obliged, butler-fashion, and Chris smiled grimly at the two-faced obsequiousness of his brother's manner. "Everything I say goes. You say nothing, do nothing, except what I tell you."

"Anything you say."

Chris threw the drink to the back of his throat. "How much cash is there in the company's coffers?"

"None."

"What about the bank account in Concho Springs?"

"Got used up."

"What the hell on?"

"Barb-wire and stuff for the ranch."

"Like hell. Catting around, booze and pasteboards."

Rufus grinned. "That as well. But that's water under the bridge. I'm a reformed man, Chris. I've learned my lesson."

"I believe that when I see it." He put his elbows on the desk and steepled his fingers. "OK, we need dough to build up a new crew and a new herd. So first off we sell our enterprises in town."

Rufus's face stiffened. "Ain't no call for that. What about the money you got for the herd up at Abilene?"

"So that's why you sent Spike out to bring me back: to get your hands on the sale cash."

"No, I thought that . . . "

Chris butted in with loud tuts. "You're forgetting our bargain already. I make the decisions."

Rufus acquiesced with a nod.

"There *is* some left over from the sale," Chris went on, "but that stays where it is as a back-up. Only for use as a last resort."

"Just for the record, where exactly is it?"

"There you go again, trying to muscle in. This ain't gonna work, Rufus."

"Sorry."

"OK. I figure some of the drovers will have returned to Concho Springs. If some have and we can get hold of 'em we'll have the seedcorn for a reliable crew. Then we send them south to buy stock."

"I knew you could handle it."

"Hang on before you start celebrating, there's more. We drop Ruddock off our payroll and see if we can get the townsfolk to start up proper elections again. And we don't tax folk for trying to earn an honest penny. If we're gonna get the Circle S back on its feet we're gonna need all the co-operation we can get. Doing right by the townsfolk should help in that direction."

21

THE bank teller adjusted his cuff guards as he approached the counter. "You only just made it, Mr Shard. We're about to close. What can I do for you?"

Chris pushed an assortment of bank drafts and bills under the grill. "Like to deposit this in a new account in my name. Bracket Circle S after my name, but only I am to draw on it."

"I'll make a note of that, sir."

The teller wrote the instruction on a form then proceeded to count the proffered assets. "Two thousand four hundred dollars," he said at the end of the exercise. "Is that what you make it, sir?"

"On the button, pilgrim." He watched while the man completed the paperwork, then tucked the resulting receipt into his wallet. "Remember: only I am to have access to the account."

"Yes, sir."

The teller glanced at the clock, moved round the counter and accompanied his customer to the door. "Good day, sir."

Chris touched his hat and stepped out onto the boardwalk. He remained there for a moment, looking along the main drag, savouring the experience. For the first time in a long spell he felt clean on the streets of Concho Springs. The Circle S was on its way to becoming a respectable outfit once again, the way the old man wanted it.

The younger Shard had given Ruddock notice to quit pending elections. And this time it was for real with no Rufus and his hardcases to foul things up. Then folks had been told there would be no more demands from the Circle S for the infamous 'taxes'. And he'd just sold the last of the outfit's enterprises. Got a reasonable price on all of them; with the money from the cattle sale, the total should be enough to fund the Circle S's regeneration.

Everything was going well. Could it be as easy as this? He knew the answer was no. For all his smiles and acquiescence, Rufus was ill-ballasted cargo. Unpredictable, like loose freight, capable of shifting violently and throwing the whole shebang off course.

For a start he was still drinking and whoring. So much for turning over a new leaf. Chris would just have to keep a weather-eye on him.

★ ★ ★

Beth sat at the window of the Hourglass ranch-house, her eyes rimmed with tiredness. She didn't know how long it had been since she had seen dawn break across the plain. As so often happened Frank had been out all the previous day and come nightfall she had retired to an empty bed. Some time in the early morning she had woken and, finding herself still alone and unable to get back to sleep, had wrapped herself in a dressing-gown to make coffee. The cold dregs remained in the cup before her.

She was on the point of making a fresh cup when she spied a shape on the road leading to the ranch-house. She watched her husband ride slowly in. When he pulled to the side and disappeared from view to stable his horse she looked at the clock. Half past nine.

It wasn't long before she heard his boots on the porch and the door opening and closing. He would have passed her on the way to the kitchen had she not spoken.

"Good morning, Husband."

He came to a momentary halt and glanced her way. "Oh, it's you."

She sighed softly. "Who d'you expect it to be?"

"You're up early," he said, resuming his journey towards the kitchen.

"I've been up a long time," she shouted after him.

She listened to the clatter of porcelain

and then followed him to stand in the doorway. "It can't go on like this."

"What you talking about?" he said, as he put the coffeepot on the stove.

"Where have you been till this time?"

"I told you, business."

"What kind of business takes all night?"

He grinned. Then, "A woman shouldn't ask her man too many questions."

"This hasn't turned out like I expected, Frank. Not one bit. A woman needs loving from a man. Half the nights you aren't here. And when we do share the same bed, well . . . "

Unspeaking he carried on with his tasks.

"All you want me for is to bring you your cornbread and buttermilk," she continued. "Apart from that I'm nothing more than an ornament."

"You always slide past the point, woman, never hitting it on the nose."

Resolution tightened the contours of her pretty face. "All right I'll hit it on the nose. You're not the man who courted me. The man who came calling at the Circle S to take me on buggy rides. All sweetness and light and flowers. Since you got a band around my finger you've changed."

"That's the natural way of things with folks who get hitched."

"No it's not. Not all of them."

With the coffee beginning to hiss, he filled a basin with water. Then took off his jacket and shirt.

She watched him as he attended to his toilet. Scratch marks were plainly visible down his back as he bent over the basin.

"So that's the business," she said.

"What the hell you on about now, woman?"

"Your back looks like you took a roll in barb-wire."

He straightened and tried to see what had caught her attention. Unsuccessful he returned to his ablutions. "Maybe I have."

"Those are woman marks. Fresh.

And not made by me." She slumped into a chair. "Confirms what I've guessed for a long, long time."

"You're letting your imagination run away with you," he said as he dried himself.

"Frank, why did you marry me?"

He completed his task, hefted the towel in his hand and gave her a tight-lipped smile. "Ain't it obvious?"

"I've been up most of the night. I'm tired. You're going to have to spell it out."

"I needed leverage with the Circle S. You fitted the bill."

"So there wasn't any love?"

"Be realistic, woman. You were my bargaining power. Water rights, grazing rights."

"So that was it."

"Worked didn't it? I got privileged status with your brother's outfit. Anyways, don't matter no more. Not since Chris Shard's taken over the Circle S. He's opening up the range and allowing free access to water, just like the old man did."

He staggered off to bed and she remained sitting at the window.

Chris was back! And in charge of the Circle S! This changed the complexion of things. She couldn't blame Frank for using her. She had used him. She'd needed to get away from the nightmare of the Circle S and seen a loveless marriage as the way out. She had thought that maybe Frank and she could work something out, but she could see now that that was impossible.

But now that Chris was back it didn't matter.

Time to think again.

* * *

Rufus lurched out of the saloon into the night air. He'd had a bad time. He was the kind of man who didn't like to be alone. Now his pards had gone he only had Spike for company and he'd not seen him since the afternoon. He fumbled at the reins on the hitchrail.

"Evening, Rufus."

He turned blurry eyes to see who it was, and said "Spike" when he recognized his sidekick in the shade of the awning. "Where in tarnation have you been, *amigo*?"

Spike gestured across the street. "The drinking parlour over there."

"What's got into you?" Rufus wanted to know. "I thought we were buddies?" Getting no answer he added, "Come on, let's get back home."

"I ain't going back to the ranch, Rufus. I got a place in a rooming-house in town."

"What the hell you talking about? Rooming house in town? What's wrong with your bunk at the ranch? There's enough spare room in the bunkhouse now the others have lit out. What's the matter? Ain't it got enough fleas for you now?"

"Listen, we gotta talk," Spike said. He nodded towards the alley alongside the saloon. Rufus followed him into the darkness.

"What's this all about? Bedding in town, not having an evening drink with me."

"Time to face facts, Rufus. The making-hay days are over. Thed, Moses and the other guys who vamoosed had got it right. A guy's gotta know when to split."

The other shook his head in an attempt to clear it. "No, Spike. We just gotta bide our time, is all. I told you my plan. Huh, you don't think I invited the milksop back so he could take over permanent? We lie low, bide our time."

"For what? What's at the end of it? Ain't no rainbow nor pot of gold."

"Oh yes, there is. When Goody Two Shoes has got the outfit back on its feet we can get rid of him and put the squeeze on the town again. Just like before."

"No, the gravy train's passed on; it's way down the track. As far as I'm concerned it's time for pastures new."

"You wouldn't leave me?"

"I would and I am. That's why I've took a bunk at the rooming-house. I've thought it over and made up my mind. I'm hitting the trail."

Rufus splayed out his hands. "So you've just moseyed over to say *adios*?"

"Yeah. But there's something else. As I'm pulling up my picket pin I need a grub stake."

"Where you gonna get that?"

"From you."

Rufus laughed. "You're riding a bum steer asking me. I'm down to cents."

"I'm not talking about cents. More like a grand."

Rufus grunted in disbelief. "You're loco."

"You owe me, Rufus. I stood by you thick and thin. Even after the others lit out. It's only what I deserve. You can get it."

"Where from?"

"Your brother's loaded. I been keeping my eye on him. That's what set me thinking. Today he creamed off over two grand from selling off the Circle S enterprises."

"Yeah, and he banked it in an account I ain't got access to."

"Then there's the dough he got from selling the cattle."

"God knows where he's stashed that."

"The point is there's plenty of jack in the kitty. If you have to, you can find a way of getting your mitts on some of it."

"My hands are tied, Spike."

"I'm serious, Rufus."

"How serious?"

Spike paused. "If you don't get me what I want so that I can get out of this rat-hole with some folding stuff in my saddle-bag . . . " He paused again, before completing his sentence, "I'll tell your brother and the county law how Pascal and Magee took the big jump."

"You wouldn't."

"When I'm up against the wall I'll do anything. You know that, Rufus."

Rufus was managing to sober himself up. "Yes, you would."

"So, you get the money — a grand is all I want, I don't care how you get it — and you and me part as pardners."

"Pardners!" Rufus was fit to explode but he didn't speak further, using the time to contain himself. When he did speak he managed to force some calmness into his voice. "OK. I'll see what I can do. Like you say, if you're leaving it's only right you should have compensation. Kinda like a gold watch for long service."

Spike relaxed. "Yeah, that's it. We're two of a kind. I knew you'd see it my way."

"OK," Rufus sighed in apparent acceptance of the whole thing, "I'm sorry it has to end this way, but you gotta look after your own interests. I can understand that. Now, you get back to the rooming-house and I'll let you know what I can pull out of the bag. Gotta give me time, is all."

Despite Rufus's demeanour Spike knew his boss of old and stepped back slowly without turning his back on him. Only when he was several paces away did he finally turn to head out of the alley. But that was insufficient precaution.

The conversation had sobered Rufus up more effectively than a couple of mugs of black coffee and, pulling his knife, he leapt at his former comrade before the fellow had cleared the alley.

Spike pitched forward with a handle protruding from his shoulder blades level with his heart. Rufus stood over him in the darkness. "Doublecross me, would you, you pissant? Play the canary to my damn stepbrother, would you? Well, this is the only parting gift you'll get from me." With that he twisted the knife savagely one way and the other several times before withdrawing it. He studied the still form of Spike, satisfied himself he was dead, then wiped the blade clean on the man's vest back.

He walked slowly to the end of the

alley and peered into the street. He was lucky. At that moment there was no one about. He moved to his horse, unhitched it and headed quietly out of town.

22

LIFE is the most precious of commodities, higher in value than greenbacks or gold watches. It is the order of things that a creature will hang on grimly to the merest of threads. And so it was with Spike. The blade had missed his heart but sliced through his lung and the twisting of the blade had added to the internal bleeding.

Rufus had heard no breathing from his victim. But darkness had proscribed any close examination. In his haste and with his own heavy, agitated breathing masking any more subtle sounds Rufus had made the wrong diagnosis.

Scraping together almost non-existent energy reserves, Spike hauled himself slowly along the alley, blood and spittle trailing from his slack mouth. After what seemed an eternity he made the end, dragging himself clear of the profound darkness.

It was a couple of punchers who found him minutes later, his attempts to crawl reduced to ineffective tremors.

"Like to know what he's been drinking," one chuckled.

The other saw the blood. "Christ. Fetch the doc."

His companion bent down and examined the blood-lipped face. "That's one of the Circle S mob," he said standing up. "Hell, let the bozo stew. Them coyotes ain't worth helping."

"I said fetch the doc. Move it. We can argue the whys and wherefores afterwards."

The standing one capitulated and set off reluctantly on the errand. The one remaining eased off Spike's vest. He ripped away the red-soaked shirt and located the wound. Taking off his bandanna he held it hard against the lesion, keeping the stricken man face-down.

"Who did it?" he asked.

Spike's face was pressed sideways into the dust. He coughed; then blood and the name "Rufus" leaked from his lips. Weakness and the awkward pressure on his jaw made the faintly delivered word almost indecipherable. "Rufus."

"You say Rufus?" the man checked. "The big cheese from the Circle S?"

Spike breathed a spluttered, "Yeah".

"Well, you hang on there, pardner. Doc's on his way."

"Listen, I got a message," Spike managed, his eyes still closed.

"Don't do any more talking. You've said enough. You must know you're in a bad way."

"That's why you gotta listen." Pause. "Before I croak."

The man in attendance said nothing and looked down the street in the direction of the doctor's place.

"Tell Chris Shard," Spike went on slowly, talking into the dust, "that it was Rufus that killed his old man. That's why he's done for me."

"You ain't done for, pardner," the man said. "Here's the doc coming now."

The medic, shirtless and with hastily pulled on jacket and trousers, made his way to the scene and knelt beside the stricken man.

"That the doc?" Spike said when he heard a new voice.

"Yes," the doctor said and gently began to move the balled-up bandanna so he could see the damage. "Now keep still and don't speak."

Spike ignored the instruction and repeated his message.

"I heard you," the doctor said, "no need to talk anymore." To the other two he said, "You carry him across to my surgery while I walk alongside staunching the wound."

They started their short journey with a living burden; but it was a dead one that they eventually lowered onto the surgery table as the doctor immediately ascertained. He made a few routine checks then found a sheet which he draped over the remains.

One of the men was ashen-faced. "Ain't ever seen a dead man before. I need a drink."

"I think we all could do with one," the doctor said, and led them to another room where he took a bottle and glasses from a cupboard.

"Anyplace else," he said, "I would report the death to the coroner and what the dying man said to the sheriff. We ain't got a coroner and since last week we been without a sheriff."

"Ruddock wouldn't have been any use," one of the men said. "He was on the Shard payroll. You think he was telling the truth, about Rufus being responsible for killing Mr Shard?"

The doctor's mouth down-turned like one about to draw a conclusion that is not one hundred per cent certain but is the best in a man's experience. "Ain't never known a man yet to lie on his deathbed."

The man sipped his drink contemplatively. "I reckon we gotta honour the fellow's dying request and pass on the message."

The doctor shook his head. "To Chris Shard? No, that could lead to more bloodshed and we've had enough of that already."

"They could both kill each other. Both the remaining Shards out of the way would solve the town's problems."

"Chris Shard is a cowman. He'd just be gunned down if he challenged his stepbrother. That would be no good. Chris is a regular joe. So far he's been the only restraint on the madman. Look how he's stripped the Circle S's power. Got Rufus on a short lead."

The doctor took another drink. "We'll do this properly. Don't tell anyone what you've heard. As I've said, that could lead to a bloodbath. Keep quiet about it. I'll telegraph the county seat and ask them to send a lawman. There's been enough killings to warrant an official investigation. And this time we've got three witnesses to a dying man's statement as to the culprit.

I don't know about the law but that should amount to something."

He looked at the other two. "Do we all agree on the course of action?"

They nodded.

"OK," the doctor said. "One more drink and we'll call it a night."

★ ★ ★

Beth had left the ranch unseen, for the first mile keeping to the brush as much as possible so Frank could not see her. If he had seen her he wouldn't have tried to persuade her to stay — she knew that — but he might have made trouble, just for the hell of it. He was like that; it was just one of the many things she didn't like about him. So, before sun-up, while her husband was still snoring his drunken head off, she had risen, donned Levis and taken a horse from the corral. She had nothing save for a few dollars in her wallet and some trinkets in the saddle-bags. She wanted nothing to remind her of an unhappy marriage.

At first she'd headed for the Circle S. It was natural; that was home. She longed for Chris. Dear, sweet, loyal, uncomplicated Chris. After a time she reined in to rest her horse. Allowing the animal to graze she sat under a cottonwood and dabbed on some scent while she put her mind to things.

A thought struck her. What if Chris was out on the range and so wasn't at the Circle S when she arrived? In her state, she couldn't face Rufus alone, along with all the trouble he was likely to have around his neck. What was she to do? She had committed herself to leaving Frank so there was no going back, not that it was an option.

The more she thought about it the more she figured the best thing was take a room in Concho Springs. She had enough dollars for that. That way she could find out what was going on at the Circle S without riding into some unknown situation.

Having decided on her new plan she

237

mounted up and headed for the town.

Light was fading when she finally made it. She quartered her horse at the livery and registered at a hotel. Over breakfast next morning she learned of the night's happenings in town.

23

CHRIS stepped down from the leather shed, hefting his saddle. Around the corral his new crew were making their own preparations to ride. Today was the day they were to head south in the first phase of raising a new herd.

Despite his burden there was a jauntiness in his step as he crossed the open space towards his waiting horse. The new beginning was starting here.

"Everything aboard?" he shouted as he passed Cy loading the supply wagon.

"Nearly finished, boss."

Chris had just set his saddle in place when a rider cantered onto the busy scene. Chris vaguely recognized him as a guy from town.

"Howdy, pilgrim," Chris said, dropping the saddle flap over the cinch. "Another one to sign on, I hope. Could do with one or two more."

The man reined in close to the range boss and leant on his saddle horn. "Ain't come for punching, pardner. Never worked outside of a store." Then he looked about nervously. "Where's Rufus?" he went on, in a voice as low as he could manage and still be heard above the general hubbub.

"Dunno. In town as usual, I figure. What is it, pilgrim?"

"Just thought I'd tell you. There was an incident in town last night. Rufus's sidekick got knifed."

Chris stopped in his task of checking the bridle. "Spike?"

"Yeah, that's him."

"How is he?"

"Dead."

Chris's face became grim. "They know who did it?"

"He managed to speak before he bucked out. Said it was Rufus hisself what done it."

"Rufus killed his own messmate?"

"Seems they had an argument."

Chris pondered on it. "Damn fool. Well, he's cooking his own goose, the mad bozo. Anybody doing anything about it?"

"No. But that ain't the point. There's more. I rode out to tell you that he said Rufus did it because he was threatening to tell you something."

"Spit it out then. What was he threatening to tell me?"

"Said wanted you to know that it was Rufus killed Old Man Shard."

The blood left Chris's face and he started to shake.

Cy dropped his last armload of wood on the wagon and hobbled close. "Calm down, Chris. Let's think about this."

Chris breathed deep. "Ain't nothing to think about." He gripped his saddle horn. "Unsaddle, boys. Trip's postponed."

Cy tried to restrain Chris as he mounted up. "Don't do anything foolish, Chris. It's about time we called in outside law. They can handle it."

"Not like I can."

Cy saw he was getting nowhere. "OK. I'll get some of our regular boys to ride with you."

"Me for a start," shouted Deuce, walking forward.

"No you don't, Cy," Chris said firmly. "Nor you, Deuce. This is strictly family business." With that he spurred his horse and shot towards the Circle S arch that spanned the wagon road to town.

The visitor made to follow but Cy caught his mount's bridle. "Why are you so eager to see Chris in a box? Riding all the way out here just to stir things up."

"Listen, old-timer, I'd ride a lot further to see that Rufus get his humble-come-tumble. Name's Connors. Used to work for Stacy Magee in his general store. When Rufus and his coyotes killed Stacy and burned down the store, they not only killed my boss, they took away my job. Have to rely on *amigos* to buy me drinks of an evening now. I

242

liked Stacy too. Good guy. Wiped him out they did, just 'cos he had the sand to stand up to 'em."

"I appreciate your feelings but ain't no reason to put Chris at hazard. He ain't never aimed a Colt at a man before."

"Don't worry, mister. The way Rufus drinks by this time he'll be juiced up. That'll balance the odds."

★ ★ ★

Hitching his mount at the first rail, Chris strode down the street, a scene darkening under an overcast sky. Somewhere, distant thunder rumbled. Oblivious, he stepped up onto the boardwalk and thrust open the batwings of the first saloon he came to. "Rufus!" he bellowed.

Many faces looked at him, but not one belonging to his stepbrother. He continued along the wooden planking, repeating the act at the entrance to each drinking-parlour.

By the time he was half way down the drag, folks were coming from saloons to his rear, knowing what was in the offing and trailing him like the wake of some boat. The rataplan beat of a piano subsided and he was about to push open yet another set of batwings when a voice echoed between the false fronts. "Looking for me, kid?"

He stopped in his action and looked ahead to see Rufus, a block on, the batwings of a saloon swinging behind him.

Dryness sandpapered Chris's throat and his belly tightened. "Yeah." He breathed deep in resolution and resumed his advance to the end of the boardwalk. He stepped sideways into the street and determinedly progressed along the hard, rutted road.

Rufus watched him, then stepped from under the awning to take up a position in the drag.

Chris came to a standstill some fifteen feet away. "You know what I'm here for. Go for your gun, Rufus."

"You know I'm quicker on the pull, kid," the other sighed. "And my slug goes where I place it."

"Don't talk. Prove it."

Rufus stood in an attitude of unconcern. "We both knew it would have to come to this one day. But, must admit, gutsy as you are, didn't figure you'd have the sand to bring the fight to me like this. Head to head, barrel to barrel."

"Had something to push me. Learning that it was you salted down the old man."

Rufus shook his head. "Can't take the credit."

"No, figure you wouldn't do it direct. Got one of your boys to do it. Makes no never-mind. You either did it or you was instrumental. I ain't here to argue the niceties."

"Wasn't that way either. But, as you say, ain't no never-mind. It's always been on the cards that one day, some way or another, you and me would be facing up like this. I could give you the chance to walk away, but I know you wouldn't take it."

"That's right."

There was a spit of rain in the air as Rufus replied, "And even if you did, you'd come back all over again. So, best get it over with. Like I said before, I'll take my cue from you. You never did get around to learning how to use an iron so I'll give you a chance. Make your play."

Chris hesitated. With a firearm Rufus was all-round top dog, no disputing, so there was only one way this was going to end; but the inevitability of the outcome didn't figure in Chris's thinking. Now it had come to decision time something else was holding him back. In all but name, this was his brother standing in front of him, the kid he had been raised with.

"You're calling," Rufus reminded him impatiently. "Show what you got."

Confusing thoughts raced through Chris's mind. But what kept surfacing above the rest was the notion that

Rufus had caused the death of the old man. Whether or not he fixed it himself, he had been instrumental. A dying man had said so, and it all fell into place. And that was the thought that spurred his hand to go for his gun.

Rufus's gaze didn't waver as his hand darted down. Up it came filled with weapon, flame tearing from its snout before Chris could apply any force to his own trigger. Chris's legs buckled and he fell back, dropping his own unfired gun.

Rufus walked over to him and looked down at the dark stain leaking from Chris's side. "Well, what do you know, kid?" he said, booze noticeably slurring his words for the first time. "I must be slipping. Don't look like a killing shot." He raised his gun, just enough to level it smack at the left side of the prostrate man's chest. "You understand I gotta end this now, kid. Otherwise, you'll get yourself patched up and come trying to throw lead all over again. As they say, no hard feelings."

He only got as far as clicking the hammer for the second and what was to be the killing shot. There was a sound like a thunder clap and he canted sideways. Bending like he'd been kicked in the shoulder-blades, he staggered awkwardly, his gun hand going slack, the other reaching for the nearest hitchrail. He fell heavily against it, dropped the gun and turned, arms spread on both sides along the rail. His loopy eyes scanned the false fronts looking for the source of the shot that had cratered his side. Maybe he saw Beth standing with the smoking shotgun. Maybe he didn't. Hard to tell as nothing seemed to register; and his head slumped forward, spittle snaking from his lips. He stayed that way for a moment then pitched forward, his head hitting the ground first so that his backside mountained upwards for a moment, then he keeled over.

The rain began to make itself felt as Beth staggered across the street, tears in her eyes. With the shotgun that she had grabbed from behind the hotel counter now hanging slackly from her hand she looked down at her brother's unmoving form. "I had to do it, Rufus. You gave me no option."

"Beth?" he wheezed quizzically. "You?" At first he couldn't believe it, then acceptance showed in his eyes. "Funny thing is, I had nothing to do with the old man's killing. The others, yes, but not the old man's. You gotta know that." He tried to chuckle but only succeeded in making a grotesque sound; and the subsequent words came slowly, almost indecipherable. "Tell the kid over there, he might appreciate the irony."

"No, don't say that, Rufus. Tell me you're lying."

But he didn't hear. Just gave a shuddering sigh and remained still.

She dropped the shotgun and staggered over to Chris. He was breathing heavily; but breathing. Rain watered the blood staining his shirt. "I had to do it, Chris," she said. "I had to do it."

★ ★ ★

Now, the rain was slanting down hard, turning the main drag into a quagmire. Rufus's body had been toted over to the undertaker's. The doctor was out on a call so Chris had been carried to shelter under an awning to wait for his attention. An old-timer had looked over his wound concluding it wasn't serious. Deuce had arrived and was standing in the rain near Doc Crane's doorway ready to hustle him over to the trail boss on his return. Beth had made temporary bandaging out of a saloon towel and someone had found a blanket for him.

"Never figured it would end quite like this," Chris whispered when they were finally alone.

"There was me," Beth said, her voice a croak, "thinking I couldn't live with either of one of you if one was to kill the other. Now *I'm* in that position. Can *you* live with me knowing I killed your stepbrother?"

"That ain't the hard part."

"I know. The hard part is can I live with myself?"

And she began crying again. Unable to embrace her he took her hand. After a spell he said, "You're a long way from the Hourglass, Mrs Turner."

"I've left Frank."

He looked across at the muddy morass that had been the scene of the confrontation. "It's a goddamn awful way to get the air cleared but at least it gives us a chance for a fresh start. You and me, building up the Circle S again."

She shook her head. "Oh Chris, it's too early to think about that."

"Yeah, you're right."

They stayed that way, silent, for a spell. The crowd dissipated, the rain kept up its momentum.

Then Chris raised his weak eyes skyward. "Grass is gonna green up."

FIGHTING RAMROD
Charles N. Heckelmann

Most men would have cut their losses, but Frazer counted the bullets in his guns and said he'd soak the range in blood before he'd give up another inch of what was his.

LONE GUN
Eric Allen

Smoke Blackbird had been away too long. The Lequires had seized the Blackbird farm, forcing the Indians and settlers off, and no one seemed willing to fight! He had to fight alone.

THE THIRD RIDER
Barry Cord

Mel Rawlins wasn't going to let anything stand in his way. His father was murdered, his two brothers gone. Now Mel rode for vengeance.

ARIZONA DRIFTERS
W. C. Tuttle

When drifting Dutton and Lonnie Steelman decide to become partners they find that they have a common enemy in the formidable Thurston brothers.

TOMBSTONE
Matt Braun

Wells Fargo paid Luke Starbuck to outgun the silver-thieving stagecoach gang at Tombstone. Before long Luke can see the only thing bearing fruit in this eldorado will be the gallows tree.

HIGH BORDER RIDERS
Lee Floren

Buckshot McKee and Tortilla Joe cut the trail of a border tough who was running Mexican beef into Texas. They stopped the smuggler in his tracks.

BRETT RANDALL, GAMBLER
E. B. Mann

Larry Day had the choice of running away from the law or of assuming a dead man's place. No matter what he decided he was bound to end up dead.

THE GUNSHARP
William R. Cox

The Eggerleys weren't very smart. They trained their sights on Will Carney and Arizona's biggest blood bath began.

THE DEPUTY OF SAN RIANO
Lawrence A. Keating and
Al. P. Nelson

When a man fell dead from his horse, Ed Grant was spotted riding away from the scene. The deputy sheriff rode out after him and came up against everything from gunfire to dynamite.

FARGO: MASSACRE RIVER
John Benteen

The ambushers up ahead had now blocked the road. Fargo's convoy was a jumble, a perfect target for the insurgents' weapons!

SUNDANCE: DEATH IN THE LAVA
John Benteen

The Modoc's captured the wagon train and its cargo of gold. But now the halfbreed they called Sundance was going after it . . .

HARSH RECKONING
Phil Ketchum

Five years of keeping himself alive in a brutal prison had made Brand tough and careless about who he gunned down . . .

FARGO: PANAMA GOLD
John Benteen

With foreign money behind him, Buckner was going to destroy the Panama Canal before it could be completed. Fargo's job was to stop Buckner.

FARGO:
THE SHARPSHOOTERS
John Benteen

The Canfield clan, thirty strong were raising hell in Texas. Fargo was tough enough to hold his own against the whole clan.

PISTOL LAW
Paul Evan Lehman

Lance Jones came back to Mustang for just one thing — revenge! Revenge on the people who had him thrown in jail.

HELL RIDERS
Steve Mensing

Wade Walker's kid brother, Duane, was locked up in the Silver City jail facing a rope at dawn. Wade was a ruthless outlaw, but he was smart, and he had vowed to have his brother out of jail before morning!

DESERT OF THE DAMNED
Nelson Nye

The law was after him for the murder of a marshal — a murder he didn't commit. Breen was after him for revenge — and Breen wouldn't stop at anything . . . blackmail, a frameup . . . or murder.

DAY OF THE COMANCHEROS
Steven C. Lawrence

Their very name struck terror into men's hearts — the Comancheros, a savage army of cutthroats who swept across Texas, leaving behind a bloodstained trail of robbery and murder.

SUNDANCE: SILENT ENEMY
John Benteen

A lone crazed Cheyenne was on a personal war path. They needed to pit one man against one crazed Indian. That man was Sundance.

LASSITER
Jack Slade

Lassiter wasn't the kind of man to listen to reason. Cross him once and he'll hold a grudge for years to come — if he let you live that long.

LAST STAGE TO GOMORRAH
Barry Cord

Jeff Carter, tough ex-riverboat gambler, now had himself a horse ranch that kept him free from gunfights and card games. Until Sturvesant of Wells Fargo showed up.

McALLISTER ON THE COMANCHE CROSSING
Matt Chisholm

The Comanche, McAllister owes them a life — and the trail is soaked with the blood of the men who had tried to outrun them before.

QUICK-TRIGGER COUNTRY
Clem Colt

Turkey Red hooked up with Curly Bill Graham's outlaw crew. But wholesale murder was out of Turk's line, so when range war flared he bucked the whole border gang alone . . .

CAMPAIGNING
Jim Miller

Ambushed on the Santa Fe trail, Sean Callahan is saved by two Indian strangers. But there'll be more lead and arrows flying before the band join Kit Carson against the Comanches.

GUNSLINGER'S RANGE
Jackson Cole

Three escaped convicts are out for revenge. They won't rest until they put a bullet through the head of the dirty snake who locked them behind bars.

RUSTLER'S TRAIL
Lee Floren

Jim Carlin knew he would have to stand up and fight because he had staked his claim right in the middle of Big Ike Outland's best grass.

THE TRUTH ABOUT SNAKE RIDGE
Marshall Grover

The troubleshooters came to San Cristobal to help the needy. For Larry and Stretch the turmoil began with a brawl and then an ambush.

WOLF DOG RANGE
Lee Floren

Will Ardery would stop at nothing, unless something stopped him first — like a bullet from Pete Manly's gun.

DEVIL'S DINERO
Marshall Grover

Plagued by remorse, a rich old reprobate hired the Texas Troubleshooters to deliver a fortune in greenbacks to each of his victims.

GUNS OF FURY
Ernest Haycox

Dane Starr, alias Dan Smith, wanted to close the door on his past and hang up his guns, but people wouldn't let him.

DONOVAN
Elmer Kelton

Donovan was supposed to be dead. Uncle Joe Vickers had fired off both barrels of a shotgun into the vicious outlaw's face as he was escaping from jail. Now Uncle Joe had been shot — in just the same way.

CODE OF THE GUN
Gordon D. Shirreffs

MacLean came riding home, with saddle tramp written all over him, but sewn in his shirt-lining was an Arizona Ranger's star.

GAMBLER'S GUN LUCK
Brett Austen

Gamblers seldom live long. Parker was a hell of a gambler. It was his life — or his death . . .

ORPHAN'S PREFERRED
Jim Miller

Sean Callahan answers the call of the Pony Express and fights Indians and outlaws to get the mail through.

DAY OF THE BUZZARD
T. V. Olsen

All Val Penmark cared about was getting the men who killed his wife.

THE MANHUNTER
Gordon D. Shirreffs

Lee Kershaw knew that every Rurale in the territory was on the lookout for him. But the offer of $5,000 in gold to find five small pieces of leather was too good to turn down.